KILLER

QUEEN

Cover Artist: Natasha Snow Designs

Editing: Proof Positive

Proofreading: Judy's Proofreading

Formatting: Rainbow Danger Designs

Paperback: 978-1-9994727-7-1

Ebook: 978-1-9994727-6-4

Say the word, and I will
    Turn around and run, run, run to you.

UBIQUITOUS SYNERGY SEEKER, "US"

ONE

MAC

BRYAN OWES ME BIG-TIME, I thought to myself as I stepped out of the shower and wrapped a blue towel around my waist. My best friend for the last decade moved out of our place a couple of weeks ago to live with his boyfriend. I couldn't begrudge him that. His boyfriend, Eli, was perfect for him, and I was *glad* they finally took this step. So, why did Bryan owe me? Easy—he pimped out his old room to a university student as a favor to his boyfriend's best friend.

I'll be the first person to admit that living alone sucks. It'd been too damn long, and I missed having someone around. Even so, I wasn't keen on having a stranger around. I shrugged off the thought with a sigh and left the bathroom, walking directly across the hall into my bedroom. Not bothering to close the door behind me, I unwrapped the towel and quickly patted myself dry before running the garment back and forth through my hair, leaving the dark-blond strands sticking up in every direction. Tossing the damp towel aside, I riffled through my top drawer until—*there they are*—my fingers closed around the maroon Calvin Klein microfiber boxer briefs that were oh-so comfy. Nothing beat being naked, but these were a very close second. I was not-so-subtly told that I'd have to wear clothes around the apartment until my new roommate settled in. These boxers were my compromise.

With it being nearly June, it was beginning to get hot as balls in downtown Chicago. In an attempt to keep the power bill down, I wanted to wait as long as possible before turning on the AC. Being naked was just as much a financial decision as it was a comfort one. All right, it was way more about comfort—sue me.

I ventured out into the quiet kitchen to grab some breakfast before I sat down to work. The cool, stainless steel fridge housed few options, so I ended up popping a Chinese take-out container in the microwave. It wasn't the best post-workout meal, but it would suffice until I dragged my ass to the grocery store.

I leaned against the woodblock countertop with my arms crossed over my bare chest and let my head rock from side to side. I hadn't planned on going to the gym this morning. I got roped into it while trying to think up an excuse to bail on having breakfast with last night's hookup. She wasn't all too pleased with me, but that didn't stop her from programming her number into my phone before I left.

The timer on the microwave sounded while I grinned at the memory of being balls-deep in… um, Amelia? Amanda? Whoever, last night. I took the piping hot container and a fork over to the table set by the large bay window dividing the kitchen from the living room. I plunked down in my usual spot in front of the window and opened up my laptop as the sun's rays warmed my back. My body blocked most of the glare in the morning, though I'd have to lower the shade by midday.

It was just after nine in the morning, and I had no idea

when my new roomie was arriving, so I scoffed down my food, threw on a bumpin' playlist, and got to work coding and building a new website for a client.

A knock came at the door around four hours later. I guess you could call it a hammer-fist or a kick based on how loud it was. Without touching the volume on the music, I pushed back from the table, scraping the feet of the chair on the tiled flooring, stood up, and jogged past the couch to the front door. More loud pounding came just as my fingers curled around the doorknob. *Be nice,* I reminded myself before pulling the door open.

I locked eyes with a guy who was undeniably related to Eli's friend. He shared her fair skin, pale blue eyes, and red hair. He was a bit taller than she was and looked about seventeen years old, which was a hell-to-the-mother-fucking-no.

"Jesus, kid, do you even shave yet?" It slipped out of my mouth before I could even think not to say it. He narrowed his eyes at me, and his nostrils flared. I guess I pissed him off. Whoops.

"Excuse me?" he scraped out. Oh yes, he was mad.

"Sorry, you just look really young. You're Eve's brother, right?" I held out my fist for a bump and died inside as his eyes tracked the movement then flicked up to mine. He tightened his grip on the bag slung over his shoulder and kept his other hand in the pocket of his distressed black jeans. I pulled my hand back and scratched at the scruff on my jaw. "Okay," I drew out, "that was awkward."

The little bastard shrugged and brushed his hair out of his face. It was tied back for the most part, although some pieces managed to remain free. "Aoibheann is my sister, yes. Now, are you gonna let me in?"

I suppressed the eye roll I so desperately wanted to employ and forced a smile to my lips. "Of course, come on in." I stepped aside and watched as he walked past me. His hair looked pretty damn long—maybe even down to his shoulders if I had to guess. He wasn't short, but he was thin and lean, which only made him look younger than however old he probably was.

I closed the door behind him and leaned against it with my hands behind my back while my new roommate stood a few feet in front of me, taking in the kitchen and living room silently. "So, I'm Mac, in case Eve or Bryan didn't tell you."

Without turning around and interrupting his perusal, he replied, "I was told." Once he had his fill of the space, he cocked his head in my direction and asked which room was his.

"Tell you what, kiddo, you give me your name, and I'll show you your room."

His nose wrinkled, but he answered me. "Dubhlainn."

Dovelin? "Oh, that's easy enough. I was kind of expecting something crazy like Eve's full name."

"It's not spelled how you think it is," he said, void of all amusement.

"Of course it isn't," I muttered. The conversation wasn't going where I'd expected it to and the kid's attitude, although amusing, needed to be checked. I'd tackle that another day. "Follow me."

I headed down the hall, stopping to point out my room and the shared bathroom before reaching the end of the hall. "There's a big closet here," I said, pointing to the double doors across from his soon-to-be bedroom. "And here's your room. It's the bigger of the two and has a small en-suite." He pushed past me and stood in the room, eyeing the bed. "Bryan left the bed for you. Because you know, he and Eli are all domestic. You'll need some other pieces, but should be okay for now." I eyed the bag hanging from his shoulder and realized that was all he showed up with. "Um, do you have more stuff?"

He set his bag down on the bed and turned toward me. "I do. I wanted to make sure I was staying before lugging all my shit over here."

"And are you? Staying?"

"I am. I want to be clear on something, though. We"—he motioned between us—"are not friends. I'm not interested in becoming such with the likes of you."

I snorted and grinned, resting my forearm up high on the doorframe. "Yeah, good luck with that, kid. I'm kind of irre-sistible."

"Is that all? I have some work to do."

I pushed off the doorframe and took a step back. I opened my mouth for a witty retort when that little fucker slammed the door in my face. A low hum rumbled in the back of my throat as I turned and started down the hall. The sound of a door opening behind me made me turn around just before I sat down at the table.

Dubhlainn stuck his head out of his room and shouted, "And for the love of God, turn down that awful music and put some fuckin' clothes on," then slammed the door again.

I sat down with a smile on my face and cranked up the volume on "Good Vibrations" before going back to work.

∘°∘

I DIDN'T SEE Dubhlainn again that day. I'd knocked on his door around suppertime to see if he wanted to order in, and he shouted back—through the closed door—that he wasn't hungry. Even so, I ordered enough pizza for both of us, just in case. Deciding to give him some space, I left a note on the counter indicating the pizza in the fridge and left his key to the condo at the bottom before I'd gone to bed.

He snuck out in the morning before I got up. The key was gone, yet the leftovers remained untouched. I shrugged and ate them for breakfast while watching reruns of *Fresh Prince* on the black leather couch. Halfway through the second episode my phone vibrated on the living room table in front of me, ridiculously loud against the glass. Bryan's name flashed up on my call display. I paused the show then answered the phone, tapping on the screen to put the call on speakerphone.

"Hey, bro. What's up?" I took a large bite of cold pizza— the best way to eat it.

"Just taking a short break out back to see how things are going with Dubhlainn." Bryan owned a small bakery he opened last year. He had more staff members now, though he still liked to spend most of his time working the kitchen. Having a pâtissier for a best friend had its perks, especially when he brought over treats on a weekly basis.

"Ah, the kid. He's, how shall I put this… kind of a dick," I said gleefully.

Bryan sighed in an attempt to mask his snickering. He failed. "Did you piss him off already?"

"Totally. I didn't say anything bad; he just needs to lighten up a bit." I took another bite and swallowed while Bryan sighed again. "He's touchy. I barely said a word to him and he already hates me."

"How do you know?"

"He all but said it before he insulted my clothing choices and musical tastes and slammed a door in my face."

Bryan snorted a laugh. "Please tell me you wore clothes yesterday when you introduced yourself."

"Of course I did," I said with an air of pseudo-indigna-tion. "What kind of person do you think I—"

"You were wearing your underwear, weren't you?" Bryan deadpanned.

A smile broke out across my face, and I shrugged, even though Bry couldn't see it. "Fuck yes, I was. He's lucky I even put those on. I'm commando this morning, in case you were wondering."

"I wasn't, but thank you for the wonderful memories."

"Your sarcasm is noted and not appreciated."

"Mac," Bryan started in his "dad" voice—the one that told me he wanted me to listen—"be nice to Dubhlainn. Eli and Eve really want this to work, and I know you don't like living alone."

I sighed because I couldn't deny his claim. "Yes, Dad."

"It's never not going to be gross when you call me that."

"Watch those double negatives."

"Don't start," he groaned.

"I promise I'll be nice to him. I refuse to get all dolled up—"

"Wearing pants isn't really dolled up, but okay."

"—although I will watch what I say around him until he recognizes my awesomeness. How old is he anyway? Is he even legal?"

Bryan said something about powdered sugar to what I assumed was one of his employees then returned to the conversation. "He just turned nineteen."

An amused hum formed in my throat. "So there will be university girls around the place? I'll be his best friend."

"Easy there. You clearly don't remember that I told you he's gay."

"And," I drew out, "there goes the dream."

"Shut up. Wanna go to the gym after work today?"

"Yeah. Just text me when you're leaving and I'll meet you there."

"All right. I've gotta go. I'll bring you some cupcakes tonight."

Score! "Thanks, bro. Catch you later."

I disconnected the call and hit play on my show. Bryan was right about the kid. I needed to make more of an effort and give him a chance to feel welcome and at home before I went "full Mac" on him. I decided to suffer through wearing sweatpants and shorts while I worked day after day.

A week went by, and I still hadn't seen Dubhlainn. He left early in the morning and came back well after midnight each day. Maybe I should have been happy that he was staying out of my hair and not making a mess in the place. Maybe I shouldn't have cared that he was dodging me. But I did—and that shit was going to stop the next time I saw him.

TWO

DUBHLAINN

COMPUTER SCIENCE WILL BE *the fuckin' death of me.* I had no interest in anything to do with computers, let alone the science of them. I sat in the back row of that full lecture, praying for the time to tick over to two and bring this three-hour class to an end. A friend of mine recommended this intro class to me and presented it as an easy way to earn one of my mandatory core credits. I was stoked to see it offered in May—and early enough that it wouldn't fuck with my work schedule—in a condensed four-week semester.

Sitting there completely fucking clueless and with a huge assignment looming over my head left me feeling utterly knackered. I was past the point of withdrawing and getting a refund, so I'd stick it out and try my best. Wasting Aoibheann's money wasn't something I'd ever hear the end of. I'd do everything in my power to pass this class if it meant dodging another lecture from her.

Dr. Bell's voice cut through my thoughts as he announced the end of the day's lecture and reminded the class of our required readings for next week. I closed my laptop and shoved it into my bag while I waited for the majority of students to clear the room. I had hours to kill before I dared go back to the apartment, so I was in no big rush.

I'd gone a week managing to avoid my new flatmate. He wasn't the worst person I'd ever met, though he was tacky and annoying as hell. I was already irritable from having to move, and wasn't in the mood for jokes. Maybe I'd overreacted—maybe not. Instead of putting up with the stress of having to deal with him, I decided to keep myself busy and avoid going home until I was sure he'd be asleep. It was easy enough on nights when I worked, and on ones I didn't, I hung out with my mates or worked on assignments. Or at least I tried.

The room cleared then I pushed myself to my feet and headed off in search of a comfortable place to work. Campus lounges weren't too crowded during the summer semester, but I wasn't in the mood for the kind of sterile quiet found where students often studied. I was anxious about my assignment and needed to relax. I could have murdered a Guinness or three to help with my nerves.

Fuck it. That's exactly what I'll do.

I slid into a wooden booth at a pub a few blocks away from school and was greeted by a waitress who didn't pay too close attention to my fake ID. I had a youthful face—twenty-two wasn't a stretch.

"Do you even shave yet?" Mac's words echoed in my head, making me groan. It truly was too bad that he was trash. He'd have been a fuckin' ride if he didn't ever speak. I never had a weakness for blonds per se, but tall guys with muscles, dimples, *and* scruff? I was pretty fuckin' weak for that.

I shook that line of thoughts away and pulled my laptop from my bag, along with my notes from class. The assignment sounded simple enough: create a website with at least three pages, photos, and working hyperlinks about a hobby we enjoy. Forget that I didn't know what content to use; I was so beyond lost when it came to using HTML or anything else Dr. Bell mentioned in class. I'd been messing around with this all week and it was hopeless. I re-read the relevant chapters three times over and still couldn't grasp exactly how any of this was supposed to work.

Computers in any capacity weren't of any interest to me. I chose sociology for my major because I liked *people*—well, no, not entirely. People on a day-to-day basis were mostly eejits. Taking a step back and looking at all of society? That made it interesting. Thinking about that wasn't going to help me with this assignment.

I slouched back against the wooden booth and smiled up at the waitress as she set my pint on the table. It had decent head on it, for which I was grateful. I handed her a ten and smile, waited until she walked away, then swallowed half of the glass in one go. *Americans and their tiny fuckin' "pints."* I was in an Irish pub and the drinks were *still* smaller than ones back home.

Over the next hour I read my handwritten notes as well as my textbook. The bar started to get louder as more people floated in for dinner. For how quiet students were in campus lounges and libraries, they were equally as loud in all bars near the school. I knew I wouldn't get anything done with how rowdy the place was getting, so I packed up my stuff, drained my second pint, and headed home. *Home? Not quite, but it's better than being in my sister's spare room.*

I stepped off the elevator and heard a faint pulse that intensified the closer I got to my flat. I sighed and reached into my pocket for my keys. *I guess he's home.* I cracked my neck from side to side, unlocked the door, and stepped inside.

I had to hand it to whoever designed this building: the soundproofing was pretty damn great. With the door open, my ears were *assaulted* with Outkast's "So Fresh So Clean." I quickly found Mac, typing away on his MacBook Pro at the table by the kitchen. The bastard still barely had any clothes on. He looked up from his screen when I slammed the door behind me, his smile shining brighter than any light in the place—and he had nearly all of them on.

He turned the music down enough that I could hear myself think again and pushed back from the table to stand. On his way over to me he ran a quick hand through his messy blond hair, not really taming it at all. I hated that my eyes tracked the way the muscles in his chest and arm shifted with the movement. I also hated the sexy-as-sin smile he was pinning me with as he approached. Why hadn't I noticed the dimple in his chin before? The bastard.

Mac walked right up to me and stepped into what I considered to be my personal space. I reflexively took a step back and bumped into the door. He extended his left arm and placed his palm flat against the door next to my head—his smile now one that gave him an air of deviousness. My heart pounded in my chest as I tried to reconcile what was happening. I could smell vanilla mixed with his raw, masculine scent, creating a combination that made me wonder how he tasted. I felt trapped, yet I was free to shimmy away to the right had I really wanted to. Clearly, I didn't.

"Fancy seeing you here," Mac said to me in an almost singsong voice.

"I've been busy."

"Clearly."

"Last I checked, I didn't report to you." Okay, maybe I was getting defensive.

"Meow," he drew out. He withdrew his hand from the door and held up both in a show of surrender. "Look, I'm not trying to argue or pick at you, Dubhlainn. I want us to talk. I feel like we got off on the wrong foot."

The sincerity in his voice lowered my guard enough for me to nod my head. "Fine."

"Good. Sit down and eat with me. Bryan brought over food and it's shit you like, so don't even try to say no." With that, Mac turned on his heels and gave me an eyeful of his broad shoulders and back dimples that led to his sculpted arse. *Jaysus, since when do I even give a fuck about arse?*

I shook my head, kicked off my Chucks, and followed after him, keeping my eyes to the floor in front of me. Mac pulled out a chair adjacent to the one his computer sat in front of and told me to sit. I slid my bag off of my shoulder as my arse hit the wooden chair. When Mac didn't take a seat with me, I spun around to seek him out. I found him standing at the kitchen counter, facing the living room, scooping and flinging pasta into two shallow bowls. Why he couldn't dish up dinner like a normal, well-adjusted adult was beyond me.

"How do you know I like pasta?" I asked him, thinking about his earlier claim.

"I called Eve and asked what you liked a few days ago."

"How did you know I was coming back early today?"

He looked up at me and grinned. "That… that there was purely coincidental. I was going to bombard you with an early breakfast one morning before you were able to sneak out."

I scoffed at that. "I do not sneak."

"You so fucking sneak. You practically tiptoe out of here at sunrise."

"Clearly not if you can hear me," I mumbled.

"I'm not deaf, in case you were wondering."

"Jeez, coulda fooled me. What other reason do you possibly have to play your outdated music so loud?"

Mac gasped in an over-the-top show of mock-offense as he picked up the bowls and walked over to the table. He set one down in front of me and said, "Don't knock the classics, kid," before continuing on to his spot in front of his computer.

"Okay, Iron Fist."

"Hey, don't knock Iron Fist, either. He's awesome."

I picked up my fork and twirled it through what looked like linguini with tomato sauce and veggies. It smelled deadly and looked just as good. "So awesome that he got his arse canceled?" I was taking the piss out of him when he said he wanted to talk, but he called me "kid" again and I was feeling more than a little petty about it. The tanginess of the sauce was a pleasant surprise; almost enough to drown out Mac's whines and protests about how great of a character Danny Rand was.

I raised an eyebrow at his mini rant but didn't otherwise reply, focusing on the meal in front of me. After a few minutes of an enjoyable silence between us set to "Shoop," Mac looked up and took a drink of what I hoped was water. "So, what are you kids into nowadays?"

"Fisting."

He snorted a laugh and went back to alternating between eating and typing. Once again, I let the silence hang.

Too bad it didn't last long.

"You're awfully quiet," Mac said without taking his eyes from his screen.

"You're awfully dependent on your computer."

"It's for work." Mac's fingers ceased their frantic move-ments across the keypad and spun the screen around to face me. *He... coding?* A series of words, numbers, slashes and other symbols were displayed before my eyes in what may as well have been gibberish. He winked and turned his computer back toward him. "I'm more than just a pretty face."

"*You* do techie shit?"

"Yeah, I do techie shit. What's with the tone, kid?"

"I'm not a kid," I all but hissed. Realizing that I needed to lighten up, I took a few deep breaths then continued. "The tone is because..." I couldn't exactly tell him I thought he was a good-for-nothing bum and was surprised he had gainful employment—not if I was trying to be nice.

"Because I look like a lazy frat boy?"

I scoffed. "Spare me. You're ten years past your prime for that." *So much for being nice.*

To my surprise, and relief, he laughed. "You're sharp. I like you." He sat back in his chair and resumed typing while I subtly eyed him eagerly. "Was there something you wanted to ask me?"

So much for subtlety. "Do you know HTML?"

The clicking of the keys ceased and Mac glanced up with a raised eyebrow. "Of course. I'm a programmer; I can do a hell of a lot more than HTML. Why?"

How do I ask him for help without sounding desperate? Fuck, I am *desperate. Maybe I could—*

"What exactly are you trying to get at?"

I grunted and smirked at his question. Despite his surface foolishness, questionable taste in music, and allergy to clothing, Mac wasn't at all the gobshite I initially took him to be. He was attentive and perceptive—I could respect that.

"Can you teach me how to use HTML? I have a due date coming up for a big assignment and I'm fuckin' lost with it all."

"When is it due?"

"A week," I replied.

Mac sighed. He typed for a few seconds longer before stopping and turning in his chair toward me, giving me an eyeful of the abs he had visible even while he sat. Jaysus. "I'll teach you on one condition."

"Name it."

"Stop avoiding me."

"I wasn't—"

"Nuh-uh. Yes, you were. I said something that offended you, and I apologize. If it happens again, let me know."

Damn him. "Okay, fine."

"Also, you have to have supper with me at least twice a week. Nonnegotiable."

"That's two conditions."

He shrugged. "I lie sometimes."

I scoffed, but we both knew I wouldn't say no. "I accept your terms."

"Beautiful. I have a lot to finish tonight, but I can start with you tomorrow if you'll be around."

I nodded. "I work until six and am free after that."

Mac clapped his hands together once and drummed on the table. "Perfect, dude. Now skedaddle so I can finish this at a decent hour." He winked at me again then went back to his task. I left him to it and took our dishes to the sink to wash.

Perhaps living with Mac won't be so awful, I thought just before he cranked up "Ice Ice Baby." *Fuckin' hell. Then again, maybe not.*

THREE

MAC

THANK GOD DUBHLAINN NEEDED my help. I hadn't quite planned out what to say to him once I finally saw him and demanded we talk. Eve had told me to sit him down and hash out whatever was bugging him, which was all fine and dandy in theory. Once I had him sitting across from me things were tense as hell and I chickened out, opting to make idle small talk instead. I wasn't particularly proud of that, though things seemed to have worked out all right.

Once I finally rolled out of my room the next morning, I found him on the couch watching bad reality TV. Curled up and dressed in a threadbare T-shirt and sweats with his hair tied up in a loose knot, he looked even younger than he had the other two times I'd seen him. He had a sense of innocence about him when he wasn't being a sour little shit.

He greeted me with a "good morning" I hadn't been expecting. It was awkward as hell, though I didn't give him any grief over it. I returned the greeting then sat down on the other end of the couch, sprawling out in the sun's rays coming through the window.

"Is there somewhere in here to do the wash?" he asked, startling me.

"The washing what?"

He sighed and rolled his eyes at me. "Washing clothes. Laundry."

"Ah. In the shared bathroom."

"Is there a particular reason why you don't wear clothes, then?"

"Comfort, mostly. I'm only wearing these"—I tugged on my black boxer briefs—"because you're new here. You missed my pajama pants this week when I was trying to be nice. Never. Again. There was way too much material constricting me. I suffered for nearly a week, and you didn't even show up."

"Are you expecting an apology?"

I scratched my hip under the band of my boxers and shook my head. "Nah. I'm just letting you know how it's going to be and what you can expect. The music isn't going away, either. It helps me stay focused when I work. However, I can lower the volume when you're home if you have something you need to concentrate on. That okay with you, dude?"

Dubhlainn nodded then turned back to the TV. "That's fair."

"Cool beans." I pushed myself up from the couch, circled around it, and walked over to the fridge. I opened the door and pulled out the milk then grabbed a bowl from the cupboard. I hesitated in closing the door when a thought occurred to me. "Hey, you want a bowl of Froot Loops?"

Dubhlainn turned on the couch, bracing his hand on the back of it. "That sugary stuff?"

I held up the box and shook it. "The one and only."

"Fuck yes. We didn't have that in Ireland when I was a

growing up. Aoibheann wouldn't let me have it when I moved to America."

I took another bowl down and filled both with the unnaturally vibrant cereal. "Shit, you're in for a treat." I poured the milk in our bowls, tossed in some spoons, and made my way—carefully—back to the couch. I handed Dubhlainn his bowl before I sat down and turned toward him. I watched him take his first bite and smiled at the look of pure ecstasy that overtook his features. We each had two bowls before I got dressed and drove to the gym.

♢

I DIDN'T NORMALLY DRIVE to the gym—or anywhere—but it was Saturday morning and my sister, Miho, was back in town after studying abroad and traveling. I drove over to my parents' house after my workout and was surprised to see the driveway was empty. I parked my ninety-five Civic in Dad's spot, got out of the car, and slid my keys into the pocket of my shorts.

The front door was unlocked and I walked in without knocking. The place was eerily quiet—unlike how it was when I lived at home years ago. It was unusual for my parents to be out on a Saturday morning, so I didn't think to call ahead. I was disappointed that I missed them, but I could come back again during the week for supper no problem. I craned my neck and looked around the rustic kitchen and living room before calling out for my sister.

"Out back!" Her voice was distant.

I walked through the house and opened the double doors to the deck, immediately spotting Miho sunbathing and reading a book on one of the cushioned chairs. She jumped out of her chair, tossed her book aside, and flung herself into my arms, wrapping her arms around my neck. I returned the hug just as fiercely and wrinkled my nose when my arm slid on her oiled skin.

"Jeez, you're greasier than three a.m. pizza." I made a show of sounding grossed out and received a punch to the arm.

"I haven't seen you in nearly a year and *that's* what you say to me?"

I brushed her long, black hair out of her face and kissed her forehead like I have since the day our parents brought her home. "I missed you like crazy, kiddo. You have to tell me all about Prague after you go put some clothes on." I picked up her towel and held it up in front of her. The image of my eighteen-year-old sister oiled up in a skimpy two-piece was not one I wanted in my head.

"Oh, that's rich coming from you."

I shrugged and flashed her a half smile. "You'd understand if you had a younger sister." She rolled her eyes, but took the towel and wrapped it around her waist. I followed her inside and into the kitchen where she poured both of us a glass of water.

"Where are Mom and Dad?" I asked before taking a drink.

"They're having brunch with the Johnstons. Today's their anniversary."

"Shit, that's today?" I didn't want to have to cancel my plans tutoring Dubhlainn. I was just starting to make some headway with him. That and he needed my help.

Miho jumped up to sit on the marble countertop and twisted her long hair, tying it up in a messy knot with a hair tie from around her wrist. "Don't panic—they decided to celebrate on their own. There isn't a supper or anything tonight."

"Oh, thank God."

"Do you have a hot date or something?" She quirked a knowing eyebrow at me.

I scoffed. "As if."

"Whatever you say, brother. You can tell me if you do. I'm not a child anymore and—"

"Nope. I'm shutting this shit down right now. You're most definitely still a child and always will be."

She snickered. "If we can't talk about this, you're really *not* going to want to hear about Prague."

"Ew. Go away. Get dressed and I'll take you out for lunch if you promise to not gross me out."

"Anywhere?"

"Yes," I replied.

"Great! I want teppanyaki—it was impossible to find good Japanese food in Europe." She slid off the counter, breezed past me, and started up the stairs.

Her instantaneous change in demeanor at the mention of lunch was suspicious. "Did you just play me to get a free lunch?"

"Wouldn't you like to know. I'll be ready in thirty." She disappeared up the stairs and I heard the bathroom door close.

That little con artist. Thirty minutes in Miho-speak meant more like an hour, so I decided I'd take a trip down memory lane and wait in my old bedroom.

My room was exactly as I'd left it when I moved out. I'd left behind all of my baseball trophies and traces of my nerdy hobbies. My nearly life-sized poster of Jean Grey was still pinned to the back of my door, along with several smaller posters on the wall by my double bed. I wasn't big into comics or superheroes until I saw Jean in an issue of *X-Men* when I was nine. She was the most beautiful girl I'd ever seen and damn if she still wasn't.

She was likely the cause of my obsession with red-haired women, an interest that got me into an embarrassing situation with Eve the first time I met her. I snorted at the memory of me making an ass out of myself then sat down on my bed and reached under the bed. I pulled out a plastic bin and lifted the lid to see all of my favorite issues of *X-Men*. My uncle gave me his collection for my tenth birthday—and bless him for it. The books were pretty beat up, but I never cared.

I sifted through the pile until I found my favorite book: issue 101—the first appearance of Phoenix. I reread the issue for what must have been the two-hundredth time and got so roped into the story that I didn't hear Miho walk down the hall until she cleared her throat in my doorway. She told me she was ready to go then headed downstairs, her maxi dress billowing behind her. I put the comics back under my bed and made a mental note to rewatch the X-Men movies soon.

꩜

DUBHLAINN GOT home around quarter to seven while I was watching reruns of *The Office* on Netflix. I greeted him and got a tired reply. The poor guy looked exhausted as he lumbered down the hall to his room. He said he'd be out to go over his assignment after a quick shower and not five minutes later I heard him coming back down the hall.

I turned the TV off and headed into the kitchen to grab a couple of beers from the fridge before I went over to the table with Dubhlainn. He already had his computer out and open when I sat down and was digging through his bag for something else. His hair was damp and once again tied back, but in a super loose bun that was coming undone. The color appeared much darker when wet, though it was still a gorgeous shade of red. I hadn't really noticed how pretty or long his hair was before, though I supposed that was normal. It would be strange to tell a guy I just met that he had "pretty" hair.

"So, where do we start?" he asked, bringing me back to the task at hand.

"Right. Um, what do you know so far?"

"HTML is the foundation of designing a web page."

"Mm-hmm. And?"

"That's what I know about it," he said quietly.

"Oh. Well, okay." I slid one of the bottles of beer over to Dubhlainn, opened my own, and took a couple of slow gulps. "I'll start at the beginning. HTML is simply a language. It's used to build the basic components of a web page. Think of an entire, fully functioning site as a house. HTML is the foundation and the blank walls. You have the structure and rooms, but it's all plain. It's a house, though it's not anything fancy. Still with me?"

"Yes."

"HTML is the language used to build that basic foundation. It's used to convey the content that will be available on the site. Let me show you." I asked him to open the Notepad on his computer and flipped through his textbook until I found what I was looking for. "See this here"—I pointed at a diagram—"this is essentially what you're going to type to get started."

"I see that, but I don't understand what it means. Why are there so many brackets?" he whined.

"Think of what you see as letters that form the alphabet. Letters on their own don't mean anything, yet they form endless combinations of words, and once we have words, we have rules, or grammar, which we use to govern how we construct our language. The angle brackets"—I pointed to the greater and less than symbols—"are kind of like the rules. They enclose text and also dictate where it's going to end up.

We're going to start by following the basic rules of the language."

"Can you show me before I try it?"

"Of course." I pulled my chair closer to his until our knees bumped. I typed up a very basic barebones file, explaining as I went, then again at the end to make sure he understood. "It's all about simplicity," I continued. "H1 is your first header. Subsequent ones will be numbered in sequence. Then below your first heading—"

"P. For paragraph?"

"Exactly. These can be numbered as well, though it isn't necessary for what you're doing. And these last two lines of text are to close out the work we're doing, just like we did with the heading and paragraph. The forward slash signals the end of whatever segment you're working on."

"I see. How do you make it look like a real website? It's merely black and white right now."

"Slow your roll. Once you're comfortable with the basics —which we haven't finished yet—we can move on to the next step. You need to learn how to build the house before you start painting the walls and decorating, if you know what I'm saying." I winked at him and finished my beer. "We can cover more tomorrow. I don't want to overwhelm you."

Dubhlainn rubbed the bridge of his nose and sighed. "This is what you're doing on your computer all the time?"

"More or less. Okay, no, more. Always more. This is the basis of some of what I do."

"So, you just have all of it memorized? You type so fast when you're working."

"Mm-hmm. I've been doing this for nine years, outside of the four it took for my degree. I have a shit-ton of data in my head. It comes with time and repetition. I'll get you to where you need to be for this assignment—try to relax."

I went to stand, stopping when Dubhlainn grabbed my

forearm. "Can you please show me more? I'm following along just fine."

Well, I couldn't really say no to that.

○°○

I SPENT my evenings over the rest of the week teaching Dubhlainn the workings of HTML and CSS—what he'd need to make it pretty. He had a fully functioning site made up when he left for class on Friday morning, and an understanding of how to replicate it if his professor asked him to prove his work.

Working with the kid was mildly exhausting at times, but he was eager to learn and didn't give me sass. He was even kind of sweet when he wasn't being obstinate and defensive. Despite having seen him every night of the week, I was kind of looking forward to taking it easy and just hanging out on Friday night. On his way out the door—with a fuller bag than usual—he said he'd be back late.

So, there I was: sitting on the couch upside down, bored out of my fucking mind at quarter to nine on a Friday night. I was too lazy to drive out to my parents' place, and it was too late to visit Grams—though I felt insanely guilty about missing my Sunday visit with her. I tried to go every Sunday for a couple of hours, but I got caught up helping the kid this week.

I scrolled through my phone in hopes of finding something that caught my interest. Bryan and Eli were having a date night, and I wasn't in the mood for anyone else's moodiness or shenanigans. I was about to toss my phone aside and go play Call of Duty when I got a call from someone named Amanda. Curious, I answered the call.

"Hello?"

"Hi, Mac-Daddy." Her voice was inviting and sultry, instantly triggering my memory of who she was.

"*Amanda,*" I said, recalling how her auburn hair looked spilling over her back while she rode my cock a couple of weeks ago. "How are you tonight?"

"Lonely."

I shifted the phone to my other ear and grinned. "Oh, yeah? Anything I can do to help with that?"

"I can think of a thing or two."

After three rounds with Amanda, I made up an excuse about an early family obligation and left her place in Logan Square. I avoided driving in the city whenever possible and took an Uber home, just as I had to get to her place. Feeling sated and suddenly exhausted, I dozed off in the back of the car.

What could have easily turned into a scene from *The Bone Collector* ended up being a normal ride home. I tipped my driver and hauled my ass inside my building and into the elevator. It was just before three in the morning when I got my door unlocked and stepped into the dark entryway. I closed and locked the door behind me then flicked on a light. Dubhlainn's shoes were nowhere in sight, though he sometimes kept them in his room.

As much as I wanted a shower, I was too damn tired to stand up for any longer than absolutely necessary. I kicked off my shoes and headed down the hall. When I got to my door I kept going, quietly creeping toward Dubhlainn's door. The light from the plug-in light in the middle of the hall cast my shadow against the door and wall. If he was home and awake, he'd be able to see my shadow under the door. I angled my ear toward he door but didn't hear anything.

I jerked my head back when I realized what I was doing and made my way to my room. I left the door ajar and stripped out of my clothes before climbing in bed. It didn't matter whether he was home or not, especially not at 3 a.m. I knew that to be true, yet I found myself staring at the lights from the city on my ceiling, disappointed that he wasn't.

The sound of the front door closing woke me up some-time later. I sat up in bed and listened—for what, I didn't know. What I *didn't* expect to hear was the clicking of stilettos against the hardwood flooring. My curiosity got the best of me and I carefully got out of bed and crept over to my open door. I waited with my back against the wall until the footsteps passed by my door, then I poked my head out into the hall. A tall, platinum-blonde with a cute ass and some wild pants walked right into Dubhlainn's room—like she'd been here before. I didn't hear a second set of footsteps, but I could have missed them while I was asleep. *That sly dog. I thought he was gay.*

I closed my door and got back in bed. No sounds came from Dubhlainn's room—other than the obvious thuds of those shoes coming off—which I found strange. I was also creeped out by my actions; our rooms shared a wall, but that didn't mean I needed to *try* to listen to my roommate score. I turned my back away from the shared wall and willed myself to go back to sleep.

I'd have my fun with Dubhlainn in the morning.

FOUR

DUBHLAINN

I WOKE WITH A BRUTAL POUNDING in my head that had nothing to do with the music I heard and the smell of bacon filling my nose. Last night got a bit too wild, and I was sure I'd be paying for it for the entirety of the day. The shite-taste in my mouth was what ultimately got me out of bed and inside my en-suite bathroom. I brushed my teeth twice before I was rid of the awful taste only whiskey could leave behind.

I didn't need the mirror to tell me I looked like hammered shite, but there it was to remind me regardless. My hair was tangled and in need of a good wash and my skin was paler than usual. I wasn't trying to win any fuckin' pageants, so I grabbed a shirt off the floor and headed out to the kitchen for some breakfast.

I saw Mac at the table as soon as I left my room. He was nibbling on a piece of bacon, reading a book, and tapping his foot along to the bass. I hardly even noticed that he wasn't wearing decent clothing until he shifted on the chair toward me and widened his stance. I was then privy to an *eyeful* of the bulge in his boxers. I coughed to keep from making any embarrassing noises then nodded at him on my way past the table and into the kitchen.

There was a plate with bacon and eggs sitting on the counter and an empty one next to it. I turned back toward Mac and pointed at the full plate. "Is this for me?"

He took a bite of toast and set his book down, splayed out on the table. "Sure is. I can't cook much, but bacon and eggs are my specialty. The bread is in the fridge if you want toast."

"This is great, thanks." I picked up the still warm plate and brought it over to the table to sit adjacent to Mac—where I'd sat throughout the week when he was teaching me. After stabbing my fork through some delightfully fluffy-looking scrambled eggs and popping them in my mouth, I noticed some red and purple marks on Mac's collarbone. I swallowed down the eggs and flashed a half smile at Mac. "It looks like you had a good night," I said, motioning to my neck.

Mac tried to look down, though I doubt he could see the marks. He gave up then tore off another piece of bacon. "Yeah, it was a fun time. You had some fun last night too."

"Not quite the same as yours."

He shrugged and grinned. "Oh, I don't know about that. I saw your company last night. Gotta say, I was surprised."

I furrowed my brows, not quite sure what he was talking about. "I can assure you that I didn't have any company last night. I wasn't even around until well after three."

He picked up his mug of coffee and hummed while he took a sip. "That's when I saw. Tall blonde, cute ass."

Oh, no. He couldn't have seen me last night, though there he was, clearly telling me he did. I pushed my plate away from me, no longer hungry. I figured Mac didn't have a problem with homosexuality considering who his last flat-mate was. I hadn't told him I'm gay, but it hadn't exactly come up in conversation. I had to wonder if he'd take my explanation for last night as well as I hoped he would.

The smug look on his face clearly told me he wasn't going to let this go until I confessed. I licked my lips and pushed my hair back, out of my face, then looked him in the eye with my head held high. "I'm gay."

Mac blinked a couple of times then scrunched his eyebrows. "Um, yeah, I know. Why do you think I was so shocked to see you bringing a girl home?"

I shook my head and swallowed hard. "There was no girl. You saw me coming back from a show."

"In a wig and stilettoes?" he asked skeptically.

"It was a drag show. I do drag performances sometimes." I held my breath, waiting for the laughter to start, but it never came. Mac eyed me with a curious expression that almost felt predatory. His reaction confused me, though it was preferable to how I expected things to go.

He licked his lips and wiped his hands on a paper towel before balling it up and tossing it on the table. "Show me."

"Show you what?"

"Proof—the wig and the shoes."

"Why would I lie about doing drag?" I didn't understand why he was acting off. He wasn't disgusted or angry— just *off*. It was unsettling.

"I'm not accusing you of lying, Dove. I just need to see."

Dove. I blinked at him, at a complete loss for words. Whatever his motivations were, he looked sincere, so I nodded and stood up. He followed me to my room and I felt my cheeks heat. What we were doing was entirely innocent, yet I couldn't bury the thought of what it would be like to lead him down this hallway under different circumstances.

I opened my door and walked in first, standing off to the side to allow Mac entry. He stepped inside, looked around before settling his gaze on me. People often said blue eyes could penetrate to your soul, but Mac's brown eyes were doing a fine job of it. He stood with his hip cocked and a hand placed upon it. I had to look away before I made a holy show of myself and got hard or said something I wouldn't be able to take back.

"Um, my show clothes are in the closet." I walked over to the open closet door and pulled out a dark-green duffel bag. I unzipped it and pulled out the red and white four-inch heels I wore the night before. I set them aside on the floor then retrieved the black silk bag I kept my wig in. The patent leather shoes shone bright in the overhead light. I was too distracted and nervous to notice that Mac had moved in closer and was now standing directly in front of me.

I looked up and bit my lip. His cock was inches from my face and the scent of sweat and sex was strong on him. All I wanted to do was lean forward and rub my face across the front of his boxers until he begged and pleaded for more.

"Can I see one of the shoes?"

His voice made me jump. Jaysus—I needed to get myself under control. I handed him one of the shoes and unzipped the wig bag, revealing the gorgeous, long, platinum-blonde lace-front wig I'd paid a small fortune for. He studied the shoe, turning it about in his hands, silently running his thumbs across the smooth, cool leather.

I held up the wig with a sigh and he stroked it, running his hand through it and letting the tendrils of hair sift through his fingers. His eyes flicked from the wig to me, but he didn't make eye contact. Following the path I thought his eyes were on, I thought he might be staring at my hair. I had it draped over my right shoulder to get it out of the way. To test my theory, I set the wig down and tossed my hair over my other shoulder. Mac's eyes momentarily widened and followed the movement, confirming my suspicion. *I still don't know* why *he's acting so weird, though.*

He made a sound in the back of his throat that almost sounded like a moan and handed the shoe back to me. I dropped it on the floor next to the other one then flicked my eyes back up at him. "Is there anything else you wanted to see?" It was a loaded question if ever I'd asked one.

Mac's Adam's apple bobbed—something else I wanted to trace with my tongue—and he shook his head. "No. I think I've seen enough. I, ah… I have to go out today." He abruptly turned and darted toward the open door.

Shite. I shouldn't have pushed. "Where are you going?" The words left my mouth before I could stop them.

"To see my grams," he shouted back before I heard his bedroom door slam closed.

His grams—as in his granny? Did I really just shock him into making that awful lie on the spot? My shoulders slumped as I let out a deep sigh.

Well. I made a complete fuckin' haymes of that.

o°o

WORK WAS every bit as uneventful as it normally was. Stocking shelves and working the register at a Jewel supermarket wasn't my idea of glamor work, but I had bills to pay and it was easy enough. I had a full, eight-hour shift that day and shouldn't have stayed out so late, though I didn't always make the smartest decisions. My actions with Mac a few hours ago were proof of that.

With hours of monotonous work ahead of me, I had ample time to stew in my thoughts and pick apart every little thing I should have done differently. Changing at the fuckin' club would have been a great start. I was so knackered last night and had just wanted to get home. It was late and I assumed Mac would be asleep as he had been those other nights I'd come back late. I hadn't even considered he'd go out, and I *really* hadn't expected him to hook up. Why wouldn't he? Mac was hot and—even though I took the piss out of him—charismatic.

He was also straight from what I gathered. Flirting with straight guys had its appeal, though flirting with my straight flatmate? I'd have to be thick as a plank. And since that was exactly what I'd done… I sighed and cut open a pallet of breakfast cereals. Then I sighed as I stared down at a dozen boxes of Froot Loops.

Mac was still out by the time I got back close to 7 p.m. Being in the flat alone felt strange—it was way too quiet without Mac's awful music blaring. Even if he had gone to visit his granny, I couldn't help but assume he wouldn't spend the entire day visiting. He was avoiding me. I went to my room and turned the water on to heat up. I hadn't had the time to wash my hair proper before work and couldn't stand another night of it in the current state it was in.

Mac made himself scarce during the week when I was home. He spent more time working in his room and was less engaged when we did find ourselves in the same room. His eyes wouldn't meet mine, and he wouldn't sit on the couch with me, opting instead for the kitchen table or the loveseat. I tried not to take it personally and let it get me down, but it was hard.

The following Friday I got my grade back on my assignment and wanted to share the good news with Mac, only to find that he wasn't home. I changed into sweats and a tee, tied my hair back, and set up residence on the couch with a bottle of Jameson. I skipped using a glass since there was no one around to gawk.

After two episodes and a quarter of the whiskey, I heard keys rattle against the front door. I forced myself not to turn around when Mac walked in. *Friends* no longer held my attention, but I kept my eyes fixed on the TV and listened to every move he made.

Mac's breathing was harsh—like he'd just been running or something. His keys crashed into the dish he kept by the front door then his footsteps grew louder as he approached the living room. I could see him standing there with one hand on his hip and the other tugging at his wild hair. He was in a white T-shirt, black basketball shorts, and Nikes—chances are my initial assumption about what he'd been doing was correct.

When it was clear that he wasn't going to take off to his room, I cocked my head in his direction and took in his heaving chest under his sweat-soaked shirt. I leaned and picked up the whiskey bottle from the table, then took a generous gulp.

Mac cocked an eyebrow at me. "Thirsty much?"

I shrugged. "Those are the first words you've spoken to me in three days."

He winced and stepped closer. "I don't know how to say this, so I'm just gonna say it. I've had a really… unexpected week."

"What's that supposed to mean?"

"Well, if you'd let me finish, I'll tell you. God, it's hard enough to talk right now when my lungs are on fire." He doubled over then with his hands on his thighs, just above his knees, then stood back up straight. "Bryan and Eli are fucking crazy with this running shit," he muttered.

"You were saying?"

"Yes, right. This week was unexpected."

"Because you found out I do drag?"

"No—dude, shut up. I don't have an issue with that at all. I mean, yeah, that definitely contributed to the unexpected, but not in a bad way."

I groaned and stood up, not at all in the mood for this. "What are you goin' on about?"

"I've been having these, uh, urges. They're worse when you're around, but they're there regardless." He ran his hand through his hair again, messing his blond waves up even more.

Urges? Surely he didn't mean what I thought he was saying.

"I can't stop thinking about fucking you." He said it so casually, like he'd just told me we were having pizza for dinner.

"Oh, fuck off," I blurted out in disbelief. He had to be messing with me.

"I realize that there are better ways I could have said that, and maybe the next time I have a conversation like this I'll explore those other options, but it's too late for that now. I'm at my wit's end here. I've been avoiding you, yes—and I apologize for that. Now you know why."

"Go 'way outta that! I don't believe you."

He nodded and smirked. The bastard. "You don't have to believe me. I only told you so you wouldn't think I was an asshole. You know, for ghosting you this week. I'm not expecting anything from you, and this doesn't change our living arrangement. I just wanted to get it out there since avoiding it *clearly* didn't work."

"Prove it."

"Prove what?"

"You're straight, ya?"

"Um, yeah, last I checked."

"Yet you say you wanna fuck me. So, prove it." Mac held my gaze while the laugh-track from the show filled the silence between us. It could have been a few seconds or a few minutes before he finally looked away. I scoffed, not at all surprised, announced I was going to bed, and turned to leave.

I'd made it to the end of the couch when heavy steps sounded behind me and a strong grip seized my bicep, pulling me back and turning me around. Mac slid his free hand around the back of my neck, working his fingers in the loose bun while his eyes bore into mine.

"Just remember that you asked for this," I heard him say before his lips crashed into mine.

FIVE

MAC

THERE WAS A LOT GOING THROUGH my head before I kissed him. I'd spent the majority of the week working in my actual office and visiting family—I'd even spent one night in my childhood bed. I didn't tell anyone about Dubhlainn aside from Grams. She was surprised initially, though no less loving or supportive of me.

Not being able to talk it out with Bryan ate at me the most. He would have had questions—probably the same ones I had—but no matter what, he'd have listened and offered advice. We were always able to talk to each other over the years. The unexpectedness of my feelings toward Dubhlainn made me panic and flee instead of taking what I knew to be the logical route. Shit, had my faculties been running at normal capacity, I'd have gone to see Eli too. He thought he was straight before he met Bry, and although the circumstances were different, he surely could have understood some of what I was experiencing.

But I didn't do those things. No, I ran—literally and figuratively. I ran away as fast as my feet could carry me and hoped my mind would calm itself if I remained in motion. I distanced myself from the clutches of temptation, and it didn't help me one bit. All I'd done was add guilt on top of my shit. Guilt over abandoning the kid and guilt for being a coward.

It had taken me nearly a full week to come to the realization that I'd been acting like a little bitch and needed to remedy that immediately. I happened to be on a jog when my epiphany came, then ran across town to get back to the apartment. Had I been thinking clearly I probably would have ran the two blocks to get back to my fucking car and drove over instead of nearly killing myself. But, hey, no one was perfect.

I wasn't sure what I was going to say when I saw him, and I *really* didn't expect to end up kissing him. Yet, there we were, standing in the living room with him firmly in my grasp and my lips pressed against his.

He wasn't kissing me back, and I started to think he'd been bluffing when he'd asked me to do it. Anyone who knew me knew not to gamble with me unless they didn't mind losing. Dubhlainn didn't pull away from me, so I took a chance and gently brushed my tongue across his lips. He opened up for me, moaning into my mouth when my tongue connected with his. From where I stood, there were no losers in this game.

Kissing a man didn't shatter my world, nor did it enlighten it. I didn't feel any different at my core, and I wasn't concerned with that. What mattered was what was tangible; Dubhlainn pressed up against me, and my cock responding from kissing him. Feeling his dick get hard against my leg was quite unlike anything I've felt before, yet it somehow enhanced the experience. Knowing we were on the same page—at least physically—only made me want to try him more.

I pulled the tie free from his bun then curled my fingers

through the back of his silky hair and tugged. His lips were pulled from mine and his harsh breaths matched my own. The look in his heavy-lidded eyes was one of pure desire. His lips were plump and reddened from our kiss, making him look downright indecent. And gorgeous.

He was definitely gorgeous. I wasn't sure how to best describe him before, but the word was clear now. That mouth, those pale, crystal-blue eyes, and that copper hair that was more orange than brown—yeah, he was fucking gorgeous. The fact that he had a dick had nothing to do with my decision on the matter.

I maintained my grip in his hair and leaned down to kiss him again, harder than the first time. I let go of his arm in favor of sliding my hand around his waist, then down to cup his ass. And what a sweet ass it was—tight and firm with a nice curve. I squeezed him hard and he moaned again, the sound going straight to my cock, further fraying my fleeting control.

Dubhlainn snaked his arms under mine and dug his blunt nails into my back while he bit my bottom lip, harder than anyone had before. I winced then growled as I backed him into the wall—hard. The force of the impact pushed the air out of his lungs in a huff and left him momentarily dazed. I stepped back in, slipped one of my legs between his and pinned him. He rose up to his toes and I smiled to myself; I'd used this technique on women for years and it worked without fail. I just needed to work him over a bit more and he'd be grinding on my thigh, begging for more.

I pulled his collar to the side and licked along his collarbone and up his neck. His skin tasted clean and was so fucking smooth. I licked his lips in a tease before nibbling on his jaw until it connected with his neck. "Do you have enough evidence?" I rasped in his ear as I braced one arm on the wall above his head and slipped the other up his shirt.

My fingertips gently skimmed over his right nipple, eliciting a desperate cry that I *needed* to hear again. I teased the small nub between my fingers and sucked on his earlobe while he cried out and his back arched off the wall. Another hard pinch and his body came down onto my leg. *Good boy.*

He built up a steady rhythm and made the sweetest, dirtiest sounds in my ear. As much as I wanted to hear every last one of them, I needed to taste him again. My beard scraped along his jaw until my lips found his again in a frenzied kiss. The hint of whiskey on his tongue didn't take away from how good he tasted and how right kissing him felt.

Needing more, I slid my hand from his nipple, down his smooth, taut stomach, and under the band of his sweats. He was commando under them—something I'd always liked from my partners—and I didn't hesitate to wrap my fingers around his hard cock. Touching someone else's was wild—especially when it differed from mine; Dubhlainn was uncircumcised, unlike myself, which only piqued my curiosity more.

I slid my hand up and down his cock tentatively while he moaned into the crook of my neck and buried his hands in my hair. The glide from his foreskin was incredible, but I still needed more. I gave him one more tug then worked my hand around his sharp hip, then dipped my fingers down the cleft of his ass. I'd only just grazed his hole when his breath caught and he shoved me away.

"No. No, no, no, we aren't doin' this."

"I don't know, your accent is pretty thick right now, and I've gotta say, it's turning me on." I tried to step closer to him but was pushed back again. I sighed and stood my ground at arm's length. "Fine. *Why* aren't we doing this? You were clearly just as into it as I was."

Dubhlainn puffed his cheeks and released a deep breath then crossed his arms. "It's a mistake."

"Is it?"

"Of course it is—we're flatmates, and you're straight."

"Don't get caught up on the details." He laughed in disbelief, but I kept going. "I want you, and you want me. It's that simple; it doesn't need to be anything more than that."

He shook his head rather forcefully causing his hair to sway. It came down about five inches past his shoulders and was oh-so sexy. "You're not the full shilling. Fuck me."

"Hey, I'm trying to," I quipped.

He narrowed his eyes at me, clearly not as amused by the joke as I was. "What if I like topping?"

Toppi—oh. "Do you?" I asked in a challenging, almost playful tone. He'd nearly melted under my touch and I had no doubts he wanted me to do the topping, as it were.

"Not particularly, but that's not the fuckin' point."

I clapped my hands together then laid them flat in front of me. "So, what is your point?"

"We don't know each other. We don't know how things will be if this goes to shite, and I'm not fuckin' movin' again just because I couldn't keep my cock in my pants. Oh, and there's also you and your flippant acceptance of fucking guys all of a sudden."

"To be fair, it's just you I want to fuck, but I get that that's not the point."

"Stop being a smart-arse. This isn't going to happen." He dropped his hands, balled his fists, and started for the hallway.

"Wait, please. I'm going to respect your decision, even if I think it's whack, but do me a solid and keep the possibility open if things change."

He nodded. "If you can at least convince me that you're serious—"

I opened my mouth to interrupt and barely got a syllable out before he held up a finger and silenced me.

"Prove that you're serious and *not* just really horny and confused."

"You honestly think I'm horny enough to go around kissing and getting handsy with dudes? Really?"

The little shit shrugged. "Could be."

"You're... wow. Go away. I need to jerk off in peace."

He wrinkled his nose and scoffed before turning away and stomping down the hall like a petulant child. As he slammed his door behind him, I yelled, "Don't act like you didn't want this five minutes ago!" Was it mature? No. Did I regret it? Also no.

Things were semi-normal the next morning, all things considered. Dubhlainn was still acting like a moody child and scowling at me. He did sit with me at the table for breakfast, though. After some probing he told me he got an A-plus on his assignment and thanked me again for helping him. The way he smiled at me then belied how distant and icy he'd been when he first came out of his room. His attitude was cute, but I much preferred when he was pleased with me. He was almost like a kitten: innocent and sweet but could claw your face off in an instant.

We didn't talk about what happened the night before, which was fine by me. If he needed time I'd give it to him. I wasn't some lovesick teenager pining over their unrequited crush; I wanted to fuck him, and it was as simple as that. The way I saw it, nothing else needed to change. Once I found out he wanted it too I thought I'd struck gold. I liked spending time with the kid, and if we added sex into that mix it would be pretty fantastic.

All of the excuses he made wouldn't last. He doubted my sincerity and basically said I was confused. While I didn't quite understand *why* I'd developed the attraction, I knew that it was real, and that was enough for me. I'd show Dubhlainn how serious I was. It might not happen today, and maybe not tomorrow.

◦ᵒ◦

"You're late," Bryan said to me as I jogged over to the bleachers next to the baseball diamond.

The rest of the guys were all suited up and scattered in small groups, sitting, stretching, or standing and talking. "Dude, I'm only like five minutes late."

"The first practice of the year is important. We're playing the firefighters on Saturday and I'm sure you don't want to lose again."

Ugh, those fucking guys. "I won't be late again, Dad."

Bryan snorted a laugh then clapped his hand on my shoulder. "Is everything okay? It's not like you to be the last one here."

"I was a little distracted. We'll talk after practice. There's actually something I need to tell you."

"Okay," Bryan replied with clear worry in his voice. I flashed him a reassuring grin before I announced my arrival to the rest of the guys and we got started.

A couple of the guys came out for post-practice lunch and beer. It was a bit of a ritual, especially after not having seen some of the guys for months. I sat at a table with Bry, Axel, Santiago, and Maxim. They were my closest friends on the team, and pretty much in general. I met Axel a few years ago when he joined the team. He used to watch us play, and we finally let him join the team when he turned eighteen. What he lacked in size he made up in speed and enthusiasm. Having someone who could speak Spanish was also largely beneficial when it came to trash-talking—and understanding it from other teams. Santiago joined last year. He was quiet in the beginning, but once he got to know us we saw his wild side. The dude was fearless and a little crazy, which I had trouble reconciling with his day job as a middle school teacher. Then there was Maxim. I'd known him the longest and still felt like I barely knew him at all at times. He was a man of few words and loyal to a fault. He had no interest in baseball, and I had to beg him to join. Big, strong guys like him and Bry made for fantastic power-hitters. Despite my size, I preferred to keep things interesting with switch-hitting —which I guess applied to me sexually as well, at least to an extent.

After lunch I went back to Bryan's apartment. When we walked in I braced for his dog, Prince, to attack me with kisses, but she never came. When we got our shoes and gear bags set aside, we sat down on a pair of tall stools at the marble kitchen island.

"Where are Eli and Prince?" They usually came to games and practices to watch and cheer us on. I'd expected to find them at home when they weren't at the field.

"Eli is with Eve today. Samir is out of town, and they're having a movie marathon. He said he'd take Prince with him to visit."

"Damn. I was hoping to see them. Especially Prince. I mean, Eli is cute and all, but I doubt he's as good a kisser as Prince is."

He chuckled and shook his head lightly. "I know you're not here to talk about kissing my dog and my fiancé. What's going on with you?"

"Can't I just miss you?"

"You can. You can also stop trying to distract me. Come on—tell me."

A deep sigh fell from my lips. Finding the right words was suddenly daunting. "Um, well. Things have been going well with Dubhlainn lately. He stopped hating my guts when I helped him with his assignment."

"That's good to hear. Eve was so worried he'd drive you crazy."

"Yeah, well, he kind of does." Bryan's eyebrows drew together in question, and I shook my head. "No, it's not what you're thinking. I actually like living with the little dude and we've been getting along pretty well."

"So, what's the problem, then?"

"I'm not sure if it can accurately be considered a problem per se, but I kind of have these feelings now that I didn't have before." I was being purposefully vague, and I hated it.

"Feelings?"

"I'm sexually attracted to him. A lot." I paused briefly to let those words sink in for Bryan. "It's actually stifling at times," I added with an amused lilt.

His eyes went wide and I thought they might bug out of his head. "Are you messing with me?"

"Dude, I shit you not."

"H-how is that even possible?"

"I don't even know. It happened pretty fast. I realized that I liked having him around then all of a sudden he was acting really cute and we were getting along, and then—" I cut myself off when I let it slip that he did drag. I didn't know if that was a huge secret or not, but then again, this was *Bryan*. "Then I saw him come home one night in drag. I didn't know it was him, I just saw long blonde hair and assumed he'd brought a girl home. I teased him about it in the morning, which prompted him to tell me the truth." I thought back to how I felt that day, the surge of curiosity that spiked through me. I checked on Bryan, and he nodded for me to continue. "So, I asked him to show me. We went to his room and he brought out the blonde wig and the heels he'd been wearing. And, Bry, holy shit, I almost snapped and jumped on him."

Bryan gave me his best Owen Wilson "wow" then slid off his stool and rounded the island to get to the cupboards. He took down two tumblers and uncorked a bottle of whiskey sitting on the counter. He poured several shots into both glasses then slid one across the counter to me. We both drained them then silently stared off into nothing.

"Jesus, Mac," Bryan finally said.

"Dude, I know."

"And this is the first time you've ever…" He left the question hanging, but I knew what he was asking.

I slid my empty glass back over to him. "I've never remotely been interested in a guy before. You know I love you to pieces, but I'm sorry, it will never work between us." I couldn't quite stop my lips from curling into a smirk. "You're just not my type."

"Asshole," he muttered with a grin that matched mine. "This is crazy—I hope you know that." He filled my glass halfway and pushed it back over before doing the same to his own.

I nodded. "Things got a little hot and heavy last night. After being a fucking idiot for a week, I told him what was going on in my head, and we ended up making out and… stuff."

Bryan slammed the glass down hard enough that I thought it'd cracked. "Did you fuck Eve's little brother?"

"No. He stopped it before it got that far. He said it was a mistake and that he didn't want to fuck up our living arrangement. Me being straight also seemed to be a problem for him."

"Is this why you didn't tell me sooner? The straight thing?"

Another nod. "You've got a shitty track record with straight douchebags. I was worried you might see me as being one of them. Then I reasoned you wouldn't, but I was too much of a bitch to tell you at that point." I picked up my glass and sipped the fragrant amber alcohol.

"I know you're not like them, Mac. You're a lot of things, but you're not a bad person. So it's just a physical thing for you, huh? Can I guess that you told Dubhlainn as much?"

I snorted a laugh. "I straight-up told him I wanted to fuck him. He didn't believe me then asked me to prove it. So I kissed him. It was… a lot better than I was expecting. Whatever's going on with me isn't confusing me; I was hard as a rock and more than okay with everything we did. I know you don't believe in being, like, gay for one person, but that's how it feels."

"Forget what I believe." Bryan stood up straight and crossed his arms. "What matters is how you feel, and you don't sound confused or conflicted to me. Shit, Eli isn't going to believe you."

"You can tell him. I really don't mind. I already told Grams. I'll probably leave out the part where I had my hand down Dove's pants when I fill her in again, though."

"Aw, you gave him a cute nickname. You sure you only want sex?"

I shrugged. It was a damn cute nickname. "Have you known me to want more? Scratch that—have you seen his hair down? I need to get my hands in that again. He's a total smoke-show."

Bryan smirked at me and raised his eyebrows. "He's pretty cute. I'm still not used to hearing you talk about a guy this way."

"Is it weird?"

"No. It's different, yet it's still the same." He refreshed our drinks and let out a long sigh. "And here I was thinking I knew everything about you—Macalister Thomas Buchanan, you've proven me wrong."

⚬[⚬]⚬

I ENDED up spending all afternoon drinking and hanging out with Bryan. I took the train home and got off a stop early because I felt like walking in the cool evening air. The city was a gorgeous place this time of the year. It wasn't miserably cold and it wasn't so hot your face melted off and you wanted to die.

Maybe it was the whiskey giving me an even bigger confidence boost, but I needed to get home and tell Dove something. If he wasn't home I'd wait for him in the entryway. In that moment, nothing was more paramount. I adjusted the strap of my gear bag around my chest before I took off into a brisk sprint for the last two blocks of my trip home.

Reminiscent of last night, I was hot and panting when I burst into the apartment. Dove was watching *Friends* on the couch again—sans Jameson. He jumped to his feet when he saw me and asked if I was okay as I dropped my bag and rushed over to him. I cut him off with a deep kiss that I wasn't sure he'd return or punch me for. When he chose the former I pulled back and stroked my fingers through the hair that hung in his face.

"I'm not confused, and I'm not going to stop trying until I get what I want." I eyed his blown-out pupils and flushed cheeks and grinned wolfishly. "What I know we *both* want." I kissed his forehead, released him, and stepped back. "Now, if you'll excuse me, I'm very drunk, and need to go pass out." I turned and went straight to my room without a backward glance; I didn't need to look to know he was watching me.

SIX

DUBHLAINN

*T*HE BALLS ON THAT FUCKIN' GUY.

It'd been six days since Mac came home smelling like a distillery and kissed me. Again. I hated that I was still thinking about it days later. Under any other circumstances I'd have given in to his forwardness without any fight. As insufferable as Mac was when I first met him, he grew on me. He was the kind of guy it was difficult to hate, even if you wanted to. With his face permanently fixed in a smile and his floppy blond hair, he was like a persistent golden retriever that just wanted to play. He also happened to be too sexy for his own good—and dangerous because he *knew* it.

He'd blatantly gawked at my arse this morning when I was bent over, getting a bowl out of the dishwasher. I saw him out of the corner of my eye, and when I turned to him and called him out, he'd just winked at me then went back to his work. So shameless. I couldn't even be mad.

I thought more about his offer as I sat in class and pretended to watch my classmates' presentations. I'd given mine the day before and was essentially done with the class. I only showed up because of the attendance requirement.

I wanted to say yes to Mac—I really did. A hot, casual thing would be good for me after my bout of abstinence while I stayed with my sister. Mac was clearer with his intentions than any guy I'd ever hooked up with—or considered hooking up with—which had its advantages. I wouldn't have to worry about mixed messages or him falling for me. What worried me was what would happen when it finally hit him that he was indeed *still* straight—he came home with another hickey a couple of nights ago and told me all about how he got it—and things got awkward around the flat. I couldn't live in an environment like that. Avoiding it was as easy as not fucking him.

Except he wasn't making it easy.

I LEANED BACK in my chair at the kitchen table at my sister's place. Her husband, Samir, cooked mansaf, which was brilliant. It was far different from any lamb I had as a boy, but it was damn good. Samir was in the home office while Aoibheann stood at the sink washing our dishes. I'd observed that to be their routine while I lived there. Considering my sister was an awful cook, it was the best arrangement for both of them.

"Get off yer arse and come dry these."

I obeyed her command and stood, picking up the cloth and the first plate on the drying rack. We weren't big on small talk to fill space and washed and dried in a comfortable silence until I couldn't help myself from asking.

"How well do you know Mac?"

"Is he givin' you a hard go of things?"

"No, nothing like that. He recently found out I was gay." It was a lie, but I couldn't outright tell her what I was considering.

"I thought Bryan woulda told him first. Don't matter none; Macalister isn't a bigot. He's a town bike if ever I seen one, but he's a good man. Always good for a laugh too. You've got nothing to worry about. Now, if you were a woman, I'd have never let ya move in with him," she said as she handed me the next plate.

Macalister, huh? I like that. "Why d'you say that?"

A wide smile spread across her lips, and her eyes beamed. "He'd try to flah ya for sure—crazy for gingers. He hit on *me* the first time we met. Made a holy show of himself when he found out I was Eli's friend. And married."

I snorted. That sounded like Mac. "Lucky for me he's straight, then."

"As they come," she added.

I sighed—if only that were so.

∘°∘

IT WAS FINALLY Friday and the last day of my computer science class. I'd be able to pick up more shifts in July and maybe even enjoy myself in August before the regular semester started back up. Traveling was out of the question, though I'd love to go back home and visit my granny. I missed seeing her every week and didn't get back enough over the years. I toyed with the idea of moving back to Ireland once I graduated, though I knew she'd never let me do that for her. I pushed that thought aside—as I always did—when class ended.

Mac was still perched at the table, typing away, when I got back. I said hi to him on my way by to my room and closed the door behind me. I had a drag show in a few hours and wanted to leave early to hang out with some of the other queens before going onstage. I was the newbie on the scene, so I was going on relatively early at nine, but that was fine by me. People seemed to like me, and I had fun regardless of when I performed, so I didn't give a shite.

I unpacked my school supplies then loaded up my bag with the clothes, shoes, makeup, wig, and accessories I'd need for my performance. A knock to my door halted my hand while I was zipping up my bag. I called out for Mac to come inside, and the door immediately opened. Instead of coming in, he leaned in the doorway with his arms crossed over his bare chest and eyed the half-zipped bag in my hands.

"I'm about to order some food; do you want anything?"

"No, thanks. I've got plans tonight and am actually heading out in a couple minutes." I finished closing my bag and tossed it onto my bed.

"Cool beans—just checking. I'll see you later, then." He pushed off the doorframe and disappeared from my line of sight. I heard his bedroom door close a few seconds later, headed for my bathroom to have a quick shower, then left for the club.

I was always a mixture of anxious and excited before a performance, and tonight was no exception. I was set to go on in a couple of minutes and had a routine planned to No Doubt's "Hella Good." It wasn't a routine I'd publicly performed before, but it didn't have any elaborate choreography so I figured I'd be good.

I rocked from foot to foot in my black pointed-toe stilettos. The shoes were relatively new and not broken-in yet, causing my small toe to chafe. It fuckin' hurt, but whoever said beauty was pain was one hundred percent correct. My outfit was a near replica of Gwen's from the video—black pants with side laces, black-and-white bikini top, and a camo-print military jacket that fit like a second skin. I hadn't shaved my armpits or legs and was glad for the extra coverage.

When the music died down and the emcee announced Renée Steady to the stage, I took a deep breath, slipped into my persona, and made my way out to the small stage. The lights shining on me were bright while the patrons were showered in dim colored lights. I couldn't make out many faces, though it didn't matter once the song started playing.

Lip-syncing had to be my least favorite part of drag. It was worse for me with vocally dramatic songs and all that shite. My style involved a ton of energy and movement—just like Gwen Stefani. I moved around and got the audience involved while having fun, and that was really what drag was all about for me. If I wasn't having fun, I'd stop doing it.

My eyes adjusted to the lighting during the musical bridge, giving me a chance to get a look at my audience. There were plenty of familiar faces—people from prior shows, some students I recognized from classes, and other queens out of drag—but my eyes caught on someone I hadn't been expecting.

I'd know that fuckin' fluffy blond hair and cocky smirk anywhere. Mac sat at the bar and gawked at me while he nursed some kind of frozen drink that came with a fuckin' small umbrella. What I didn't understand was why he was there and how he'd found me. The song carried on and I shifted my focus to other patrons. I had about a minute left to figure out how to handle this situation before I left the stage.

Part of me wanted to leg it and pretend I didn't see him. Another quick glance his way told me that wasn't going to be an option. That bastard knew damn well I'd seen him. He was wearing a bright red tank and not even trying to be subtle. All speculation on the matter ended when he winked at me and his smirk grew wider.

The song ended, and I posed with my tongue out for the applause. Wanting to get changed and over to the bar as quickly as possible, I collected up my tips, blew some kisses, then headed backstage. I made it back to the small dressing room where I'd left my bag and found one of my mates waiting for me.

A wide smile split his dimpled cheeks when I got closer, and he pulled me in for a hug. Hugging wasn't something I enjoyed doing, though I made concessions for Taylor. He was far too unbridled in his affection to take no for an answer, and I didn't mind it one bit from him.

I rubbed my hand over his close-shaved head as we parted—I always loved the way his coarse hair felt, almost like thick stubble. His cheekbones were always pronounced, but they were contoured and looking sharp as hell now in preparation for his performance.

"I was running late and missed you. I heard you slayed out there, hun."

"I did all right," I replied as I moved around him and sat down, beginning to unpin my wig.

"Whatever you say. You're too humble, sweetie. I'ma let you get away with it, though. For now."

I snorted a laugh and dipped my head down to reach the pins in the back. "Would you rather me be a cocky arsehole?"

"Of course not. I just want you to know how good you are and own that. And don't tell me you do, because I know yo pale ass would be lyin'."

I didn't have to look at him to know his brown eyes were narrowed on me and his full lips were pursed. A small giggle rippled through me before I sat back up and pulled my wig off. I removed the awful hair cap and put it and the wig inside my silk wig bag.

"Laugh all you want, Irish. That adorable accent will only let you skate by for so long."

"Yes, Taye," I mumbled.

"Are you sticking around tonight?"

"I'm not. Something came up I have to tend to."

"Yeah, because that's not hella vague or anything."

"Sorry. It's my flatmate. He's… here." I started undressing while Taylor gasped.

"The hunky blond who wants your ass is *here*? Cancel my set. I need to see this." Taylor turned toward the exit, and I grabbed his arm before he could dash away.

"Nope. I'm going to go find out what he wants and then we're leaving. He must have followed me tonight, which is rather stalkerish."

Taylor faced the mirror and sat down with a whimsical sigh. "I don't know why you're playing so hard to get. We both know you want to ride him like a mechanical bull—but that's none of my business."

"Thank you so much for staying out of it."

He laughed then nudged me with his shoulder. "Hurry up and get changed before one of the other girls shows that man too good of a time."

Just as Taylor suggested, Sasha was giving it her best go with Mac when I returned to the bar. I sat down next to him, sent her away, and ordered a shot of tequila. Mac had an amused grin plastered on his face for the entire exchange with Sasha, though he kept his mouth shut. His silence and annoyingly handsome face were too much to handle, and I downed the shot when it was placed in front of me then immediately ordered another.

"Did you follow me tonight?"

He hummed and sipped his drink. "Sure did."

"Why would you do that?"

His smile finally gave way to an expression far too serious for how unapologetic he was a few moments ago. "I saw you packing your bag earlier and couldn't help myself. I needed to see you all"—he waved his hand in front of his face

—"done up. You didn't say you were all badass and channeling Gwen Stefani."

My eyes narrowed on him. "You like Gwen?"

"She was my first major crush until I found Jean." He waggled his eyebrows and smiled, although it seemed to be more to himself than me.

"Who is Jean?"

"Jean Grey. The most beautiful creature imaginable."

I tilted my head to the side while I tried to place the way too familiar name. "You mean, like X-men? Famke Janssen?"

"No. Famke is a knockout, but I'm talking about classic Jean from the comics."

I raised a brow and took the shot the bartender slid my way. "*You* read comics?"

"I used to. Is that so hard to believe?"

A heavy sigh fell from my lips and my shoulders drooped. It shouldn't have surprised me. Mac differed from nearly every assumption I'd initially made about him. "I guess not. So, now what? You've seen me in drag—what do you get out of it?"

He shrugged and sipped his drink again. "I dunno. Jerk-off material for a solid month?"

I was about to call him a slew of colorful names when I saw the corner of his mouth lifted into a smirk. "You're an arsehole."

"I'm a fucking golden retriever."

It was true enough. The bartender came back, and Mac ordered two more shots as I was about to ask for my tab. He winked at me and insisted on another round as a new queen took to the stage. I leaned in close to his ear and almost burst into laughter when his whole body froze. I licked my lips and whispered, "You're paying."

౸

I UNLOCKED the door for us since Mac was fuckin' bolloxed and kept trying the wrong key in the door while laughing like a lunatic. I wasn't exactly sober myself, but I at least had proper function of my motor skills, unlike the happy drunk I had slung over my shoulder—the very heavy, happy drunk.

I managed to get us both inside and the door locked before the keys slipped out of my hand and crashed against the hardwood floor—something else Mac found hilarious. I sighed and led us down the hall, not bothering with our shoes. We reached Mac's door first, and I propped him up against his closed door.

"I think you can make it from here." I thumped his chest lightly and he brushed his wild hair out of his face, grinning at me with heavy-lidded eyes that made me want to step in closer and feel his heat against me again. My hesitation only lasted a moment. I blinked a few times as if it would clear my head, then turned and went for my room.

Warm arms snaked around my waist, halting my progression. Holding me tight, he pressed his forehead against the back of my head and breathed in deep. A low moan rumbled in his throat and sent chills down the back of my neck.

"Tell me again why you don't want this?"

"I don't *not* want it, I just—"

Mac pulled my hair, jerking my head back and to the side, giving himself easy access for the kiss he surprised me with. His lips were soft against mine and I found myself chasing his mouth when he broke the short kiss.

"Please trust me. This could be so good, dude."

"Okay," I whispered. Maybe I was a little drunk, or maybe I was just really horny—it didn't matter. Right then I wanted Mac, and all of my common sense and logical thoughts could fuck right off.

SEVEN

MAC

I FROZE WHEN MY BRAIN PROCESSED what I'd just heard. I hadn't meant to beg him like some desperate loser, but I couldn't stop myself. *And now he's saying yes?* Suddenly feeling remarkably sober, I jerked my head back to get a better look at him in the dim light. "You sure?"

Dove turned in my arms and slid his hands up my chest. He fisted the front of my shirt and pulled me down into a kiss that threatened to end me. I'd been stealing kisses from him all week—quick pecks more than anything— but *this* kiss had delivered a message; a message I received crystal fucking clear.

I hastily brushed my hands down Dove's body and circled around to cup him under his ass. I gave him no other warning before I hoisted him up and against me. Without me having to explain, he wrapped his legs tight around my waist. I turned and slammed him into the wall hard enough to knock the breath out of him before I claimed his mouth in a greedy kiss.

There were hints of tequila and lemon on his tongue, as I was sure there were on mine. He tasted great, though his mouth wasn't what I craved in that moment. I hiked him up a bit higher and secured my hold on his back and ass before I pulled us away from the wall and turned toward my room. Dove wasn't exactly heavy, but he was heavier than most of the women I was used to carrying, and I wasn't going to risk dropping him and ruining this.

He pulled away from my mouth after just one step and shook his head. "My room. I have… what we'll need." His tongue darted out and licked up the middle of my lips with a slow, teasing flick.

"I bet you suck dick like a champion."

"Take me to my room, and I'll show you just how truthful that notion is."

I didn't question his words and headed for his bedroom door. I fumbled the handle a bit in the dark—*maybe* because I was drunk—before the door opened and I walked us over to the bed. Dove was kissing my neck, quickly turning the semi I was sporting in the hall into a full-fledged hard-on. His mouth felt amazing on my neck, alternating between soft kisses and licks—and a hard-as-fuck bite.

I hissed through gritted teeth then tossed Dove onto his bed, watching him scramble and sit up. We stared each other down in the dimly moonlit room, both of us breathing as if we'd just run a mile. He slowly grabbed the hem of his T-shirt and pulled it over his head. I stood transfixed as his hair spilled out and over his pale shoulders and chest. I wished we had light so I could see him clearer, but I wasn't about to take my eyes off him to go hit the switch.

Unable to bear merely watching any longer, I scrambled out of my shirt and went for my belt buckle. My coordination was still shit and it took me what felt like an eternity to just get the damn thing undone. In that time, Dove had undone his jeans and scooted over to the edge of the bed. His steady hands stilled my clumsy ones then pushed them away.

"Let me," he said, grinning up at me while he undid my belt. His eyes focused on my tented boxer briefs directly in front of him. He licked his lips and hummed appreciatively before pushing the fabric down, all the way to my feet. I swayed on my feet, suddenly feeling lightheaded with all of my available blood in my cock. Dove held my thighs and rubbed his cheeks along my cock—one side then the other. His face was smooth—freshly shaved for his show I assumed —and the drag from his skin felt incredible. He slowly pulled back until my tip was just touching the corner of his mouth, then he flicked his eyes up at me and winked.

Oh, you cocky little shi—

"Umph, fuck," I scraped out as Dove sucked the tip of my cock between his slick, soft lips. Oh so slowly, he took more of me into his mouth until I felt the back of his throat. When I thought he'd pull back he shifted and leaned in closer, taking my cock down his throat until his nose was buried in my pubic hair.

I rolled my head around then looked back down at him to find him staring back at me with fuck-me eyes. My cock twitched at the sight of him and the slow torture he was subjecting me to. His tongue rolled across the underside of my dick with slow, yet deliberate movements.

I wanted to thrust. I wanted to hold him still and use him to get off, but I kept my hands up on my shoulders, away from temptation. Whether he sensed my desperation or if he just wanted to, Dove pulled back until just my cock-head was in his mouth, then plunged back onto it, swallowing around me.

I grunted and fisted his hair with both hands, but I didn't guide his movements at all. The guy clearly knew what he was doing and I was just hanging on for the ride. He worked me over at his own devastatingly effective pace and seemed to enjoy every second of it. If I moaned, he repeated his actions;

if I pulled his hair, he increased the pressure. I'd never been blown by someone with such an attention to my reactions—it was fucking bliss. The best part was that he moaned along with me, like *he* was the one receiving the best fucking blowjob of his life.

As much as I hated to stop him, I didn't want to come without fucking him. I pulled his head back then pushed him down on the mattress. He still had his stupid pants on, so I yanked on the legs and cast them aside. My eyes trailed back up his long, lean, legs and went wide when I noticed he'd gone commando—a detail I'd somehow missed in my rush to get him naked.

His sparse body hair matched the copper shade on his head and framed his hard cock, looking all-too inviting. He flung his hair over his shoulder and squeezed the base of his cock, slightly pulling back his foreskin, while biting his lip. A bead of pre-cum pooled in his slit, glistening in the light from the window.

"Fuck, that's sexy." My body reacted and I found myself sliding my hand up his leg and kneeling next to him on the bed. His leg hair caught me off guard and my hand momentarily faltered, though it thinned out the higher my hand traveled. It was the strangest thing—I wanted to touch him. I wanted to *fuck* him, and the idea of doing such had me on the verge of coming. Yet, something as simple as touching a hairy leg caused me to have a moment of pause. It was stupid, and I pushed the thought aside to focus on the alluring guy before me, waiting for me to get my head in the game. That's all this was, after all.

I wrapped my fingers around his cock and marveled once again at how the skin glided so smoothly. I stroked him slow to get a feel for him and to see what he liked. His low moans and whimpers served as an erotic soundtrack to my exploration, and I was ready to crank the music up.

Watching Dove's face closely, I tightened my grip on him and added a twist on my down-stroke—just how I like when I jerked off. His lips fell open on a wordless sigh and his hips rose off the bed, forcing his cock through my tight fist again. I held my fist higher and he thrust his hips up into it again and again, never letting up on his cries.

"Stop teasin' me," he moaned and rolled onto him stomach, crawling further up the bed on his hands and knees. With his knees spread wide he leaned down until his cheek pressed into his pillow.

The arch of his back made his ass look like it was on display just for me—*I guess it is*—and I gave my balls a squeeze and tug to calm myself down. After a few deep breaths I crawled up behind him and ran my hands over his hips and lower back. His skin was so soft, yet he was lean and firm under my fingertips. Soft curves were replaced with hard angles and it felt different, but no less right or wrong.

I pushed my hips forward and slid my cock in the dip along the top of Dove's cute little ass, then back down again and again. As much as I wanted to be balls-deep in him, I wanted him to be right there with me and teased him a bit longer.

"Mac, if you don't fuck me in the next thirty seconds I'm going to throw you out of my room and go find someone else."

A loud crack cut through the silence as I struck his ass hard enough to sting my hand. "Don't be a brat. Let me enjoy this for a sec."

Dove groaned while I continued my measured thrusts, leaving pre-cum on his ass and back. He reached over to the nightstand and pulled out a bottle of lube and a condom then tossed them next to me. "Come on. I promise it'll be better."

I stilled my hips and picked up the condom, opening it

while I asked, "I'm no expert, but I've done this before—don't you need some prep?" I dragged my thumb down his crack and pressed the pad against his hole. "Maybe some fingers first."

He twitched against my thumb, and I bit back a grin. Setting him off was the last thing I wanted to do. "Just go slow and it will be fine. And use lube."

Fully suited up, I pumped out an ample amount of lube and coated my cock as well as Dove's hole then lined myself up. I held the base of my cock and slowly pressed against Dove, immediately feeling resistance. When I would have backed off, he pushed back and sucked in a sharp breath when the tip of my cock breached that tight ring of muscle.

"Keep going."

My blunt fingernails dug into his skin as I rolled my hips, working my cock in deeper until he'd taken every inch of me. I stilled and reveled in the intense heat from his body mixed with the sounds of his ragged breathing and moans, some of which sounded pained.

"You good, dude?"

He laughed, then winced when he tightened around me. "Don't call me 'dude' right now. Keep going."

Atta boy. I ran a hand up the length of his back and gripped his shoulder while I ground my hips into his. Going so slow was testing my self-control like nothing else had, though it wasn't long before Dove pushed up on his hands and nodded at me over his shoulder.

I pulled out nearly all the way then snapped my hips forward until our bodies slapped together. I fucked him hard and fast at a pace that was entirely unsustainable in my current state. He took everything I gave and even pushed back to meet my thrusts. I was close to coming from the thought of what we were doing. I was having sex with a guy —and it was fucking great.

I looked down at the gorgeous expanse of milky white below me and was somehow unsatisfied. I wanted to see Dove's reactions, and I was pretty sure I wanted to see his face when he came. With that thought in mind, I slowed down and pulled out, ignoring Dove's protests. I grabbed his waist and one of his legs and flipped him onto his back before sinking down between his legs.

In a matter of seconds, I was back inside of him and watching his eyes go wide and his lips part on a gasp. His back arched off the bed on the next stroke and he wrapped his arms around me, his fingers digging into my back. His breath tickled my lips and I knew what I'd been missing before.

I pressed my lips to his, quieting his moans and tasting more of the lemon from earlier. Dove turned away from it and bit my earlobe, making me wince.

"Fuck me harder," he rasped in my ear.

I grabbed one of his legs behind the knee and pushed it up toward his chest for better access, and then let him have it. My hips snapped forward again and again, driving my cock deep into him. Our harsh breathing, his moans, and the distinctly lewd sound of skin slapping against skin filled the room, resulting in the best soundtrack to further stoke my desire.

Pain worked its way into Dove's expression. He gritted his teeth and hissed while his brows drew together. Fucking him felt completely and utterly euphoric, but I didn't want to hurt him. I considered whether to stop or ask him again if he was okay. He must have noticed the concern on my face because he cupped my cheek in one of his hands and nodded before sliding his hand into my hair.

After a few more thrusts, I needed more. I sat up until I was resting on spread knees and pulled Dove's hips up off the bed and told him to wrap his leg around my waist. He quickly did as asked while I worked my cock back inside of his tight ass. With one hand on his ass and the other on his hip, I pushed all the way in to the root and nearly came when a loud cry forced its way out of Dove. It was unlike any sound he'd made for me, and I wanted to hear it again. I held him tight and drove into him again, receiving the same wanton moan. He gripped the sheets by his head and pleaded with me not to stop.

Oh, fuck yes. I shoved into him at an unrelenting pace, trying to maintain some semblance of rhythm. Sweat beaded on my brow and dripped from the tip of my nose, landing next to Dove's hard dick. My thighs burned from exertion, but I pressed on, my orgasm within reach. I couldn't come without Dove doing so first. My hands on his body felt like the only things tethering me to the ground and I didn't dare let go.

"I need you to come—soon."

Without a word, his right hand went straight for his dick. I watched him jerk himself off and marveled at the sight. The lean muscles in his shoulder and arm corded with the intensity of his movements, ultimately drawing my attention back to the source of his efforts. He stroked his cock fast and hard without much finesse.

His body lay in the shadow cast from mine, and I wished I could see him more clearly. I wanted to explore and touch every inch of him, teasing and tasting as I went. But now wasn't the time for that. Right now, I needed him to come. With the last of my stamina, I pushed harder and faster, teetering over the edge and hanging on with a bruising grip.

Dove's hand moved faster, and I heard him curse on a sigh at the same time his body clenched around me. As much as I wanted to close my eyes and let the sensation take over, I kept my gaze on him and watched as his cock jerked and shot thick streams of cum on his stomach and chest. It was the most erotic thing I'd ever seen and it was more than enough to push me over the edge. My hips stilled as my orgasm tore through me and I emptied into the condom, still balls-deep in Dove's perfect ass.

After two more lazy thrusts I pulled out, and dropped onto my back next to Dove. He'd winced when I pulled out. "Are you okay?"

"I am. Just a wee bit sensitive." He threw an arm over his eyes while his body shook with laughter. "Jaysus fuckin' Christ. I don't think I can move right now."

"Dude, same." Except I needed to get up. I had the condom to take care of and the whole not-making-things-awkward-by-sticking-around thing. My roommate and I just had sex; the polite thing to do would be to go back to my room before things got weird. And I would do just that. I just needed to catch my breath and chill for a minute.

Why am I so hot? In a sleepy haze, I kicked my blanket off and turned—*what the hell?* Something was weighing me down, and whatever it was, it was radiating some serious heat. I opened my eyes and blinked away the sleep to see a mess of red hair on my arm and chest. Upon closer inspection, Dove was curled around me from head to toe, sleeping soundly. I moved my free hand over my cock and didn't feel any mess or a condom. Had Dove clean me up after I passed out? *Well, who else would have done it, dumbass?*

I needed to leave. Falling asleep in Dove's bed was a rookie mistake and I knew better. We agreed that sex was a good idea, not sharing beds and snuggles. Carefully, I scooched over to the vacant side of the bed and climbed to my feet. I gathered up my clothes and left Dove's room, closing the door behind me and heading to my own bed. I climbed into my cold sheets and closed my tired eyes, hoping things wouldn't be awko-taco in the morning.

The sun was shining, Ol' Dirty Bastard was bumpin' through the speakers in the living room, and the sweet sound of cereal being poured into a bowl had me feeling alive and ready for the day. Not to mention the fact that I was over-the-moon about last night. Any uneasiness I felt last night had vanished and I was only left with how fucking amazing fucking Dove had been. He'd exceeded my expectations in every way, and I hoped I'd done the same for him. If he was down for more, I intended to make the next time even better —and it would be with the lights on full blast. As great as last night had been, I knew I could do better for him—for both of us.

I overfilled my bowl with milk and made a mess on the counter while my mind had drifted to all the perverse things I wanted to do to Dove. Whoops. I quickly cleaned up the mess then took my bowl over to the couch. Saturday morning television wasn't my favorite, but I put on some sports highlights, vaguely paying attention to the MLB draft while I ate my breakfast.

"Do you live off of cereal?" Dove asked, startling me.

I spun around, bowl still in hand, and grinned at him. "When Bry slacks and doesn't bring me food, usually, yes. I took a bowl down for you in case you wanted some." I turned back toward the TV and focused on the name and stats displayed before me. Dove looked like a goddamn snack, with his sex-rumpled hair and a rather sizable hickey on his neck. I'd have ended up bending him over the kitchen counter had I kept my eyes on him.

"Thank you. I'm fuckin' starved."

"Language! It's like nine in the morning."

"Feck off, will ya. Eat a dick."

"Meow. Only if it's yours." Was that true? Surely, there

had to be other guys I could be attracted to. Maybe. *Ugh. Sexuality is confusing.*

Dove sighed. I could picture him shaking his head, and I smiled around a mouthful of Froot Loops. "You're exhausting."

I bit my tongue instead of making the obvious sex joke I so desperately wanted to make. He'd just woken up. I could be patient. "If you insist."

"I do."

I turned the music down a bit when I heard more cereal sprinkling into a bowl. Dove came and sat down crossed-legged on the other end of the couch. His hair was tied up in a messy knot and he wore a well-worn graphic tee and boxer briefs. I giggled to myself then took another bite of my cereal.

"What do you find so amusing this morning?"

"I'm rubbing off on you," I simply replied.

"If that's a sex joke, I swear to God—"

"No, perv. Get your head out of the gutter." Dove huffed, but I cut him off before he had a chance to speak. "I was referring to your choice in attire this morning. Rather, your lack thereof."

Dove glanced down to his bare legs then looked away from me, almost cartoonishly. Adorable. "I need to do laundry."

"You don't have to explain. I'm not judging. Besides, it's more comfy this way. However, if you're working today you might want to wear something with a bit more coverage." He tilted his head in question, and I motioned to my neck where he had a red mark on his. "You've got a little something on your neck."

"No." One of his hands went to his neck and felt around. "No, no, no. You *cannot* mark me!"

I bit my top lip and cringed. "I guess this is a great time to discuss boundaries, then?"

"I have to get ready for work soon." He cut his eyes at me and growled under his breath. So feisty. "We can talk about it as soon as I get back."

"Ah, I might be out. I'm going to go visit my grams today."

"Wait, you were serious before when you said you had to go see your granny?"

"Hey, Daisy Buchanan is a delightful woman to spend time with. She practically—"

He held up a hand, silencing me. "I'm sorry, what? Daisy Buchanan? As in *The Great Gatsby*?"

I nodded. "The one and only. I suppose I shouldn't tell you that my father's name is Thomas…"

"Oh, Jaysus."

"Thomas is also my middle name," I added with a smirk.

"Why am I surprised? Nothin' about ya is right."

"Aww, cute, you're getting all extra-Irish on me."

"Whatever." He brought his bowl up to his lips and drank down the milk remaining in the bowl before he shot to his feet and glared at me. "You're my flatmate, so I'll see you again eventually."

He stormed off, dropping his bowl in the sink on his way back to his room. He slammed the door extra loud, which only made me like him more. *Ah, so adorably feisty, that one.*

⁛

"WHAT DID YOU DO?" Grams asked me with narrowed eyes.

"I have no idea what you're talking about."

She picked up one of the dominoes on the table and biffed it at my face. "Don't get coy with me, boy. You've had a mischievous grin on your face since you walked through the door."

I shrugged and glanced around the room, taking in the mementos from her life, as well as various photos of Miho and me. She'd moved into this retirement facility a couple of years ago when my grandpa died. Mom and Dad had wanted her to move in with them, but Grams insisted on this home in particular. Here, she had her own apartment, access to a gym with a variety of activities, and a network of neighbors and friends. Not to mention, several sweet ladies baked me cookies to take home every time I visited—perks of being "a darling and handsome grandson."

Grams raised another domino and I flinched, putting my hands up in front of me. "Okay! I concede. I did a thing."

"Do I have to pry it out of you?" she asked with one corner of her mouth upturned.

"Dubhlainn and I had sex last night." I paused for her reaction, and I was not disappointed when her eyes went wide and she smiled. "And yes, it was amazing."

"Well done, boy. What does this mean for you now?"

"Hopefully it means I'm in for a lot more of it. He's beautiful and lives with me—that is way too convenient to pass up."

"That's not what I meant, dear." She cocked an eyebrow and leveled me with her intense brown eyes. She was a petite woman and always prided herself on looking presentable, and today was no exception. Dressed in a fitted floral dress and white cardigan, nothing was out of place. Her blonde hair had turned mostly gray, but those eyes were still fierce.

"I guess I'm bisexual?" It was more of a question than a statement.

"Try not to sound so confident," she deadpanned.

"Well, I'm clearly not straight. I've got irrefutable evidence in support of that now. Bryan is probably right in saying that it's pretty unlikely to just be gay for one person, so I'm probably some degree of bisexual." I counted on my fingers for show and huffed. "Maybe ten percent. Ish."

"Are you happy with this new development?"

I thought back to last night. Being with Dove had felt right and not once did I want to stop. When I recalled how I wanted to have my way with him in the kitchen this morning, I couldn't stop the full-on smile that overtook my face.

"There it is," she said. "That smile says it all." Grams reached across the table and squeezed my hand before gently slapping my cheek. "Now, hurry up and make your play—it's still your turn."

"Yes, Grams." I glanced down at my tiles and bit back an evil grin. "You're going down."

"I've been playing this game longer than you've been alive. Quit stalling."

I pushed thoughts of Dove and my ambiguous sexuality aside and focused on the game. She wouldn't go easy on me, and I had every intention of winning.

EIGHT

DUBHLAINN

"Sis, what the hell happened to you, and where can I get some?"

I glanced down at my body and noted the fading bruises on my legs and hips. I'd noticed the mark on my neck hadn't fully faded before I got in the shower that morning. Standing in front of Taylor in nothing but my kex, I must have looked quite a mess. It'd been a week since Mac took me for a ride, and I hadn't quite wrapped my head around the fact that it'd happened. The ache in my arse the next morning and the marks that lingered were proof of what transpired, but he hadn't tried to do it again, nor had we talked about it. I was just as much to blame for that, though.

"Earth to Dubhlainn." Taylor stood in front of me and snapped his fingers inches from my face. "Wake up, hun."

"Sorry. I spaced out."

"No shit," he teased. Taylor wrapped his arms around my neck and cocked his head to the side as a devious smile spread across his face. "So, you gonna tell me who rocked your world? Or do I have to start guessing?"

"It was Mac."

A quiet gasp rushed out of him before what I could only call a squeal. "When?!"

"Last Friday, after the show."

"You bitch." He followed up the accusation with a hard pinch to my cheek that made me cry out. "It's been a full week. Why didn't you tell me sooner? That's the good tea you need to give me while it's still hot."

"I'm sorry. I wasn't trying to keep it from you. It's been… weird with him this past week."

"What do you mean? Was the sex bad?" Taylor tugged my arm and led me over to the couch in his studio apartment. It was littered in our clothes as we prepared for tonight's show.

"Not even close. Mac was deadly. He gave me everything I asked for without hesitation."

"Then why has it been weird?"

I huffed, long and slow. "We haven't talked about what happened… and it hasn't happened again. I keep waiting for him to, I don't know, jump me or something. He was so tactile back when he was trying to sway me, and so intense during. He's barely touched me at all this week, and it's weird. He isn't acting awkward around me or freaking out—he's not doing *anything* different, and that's what I find strange."

Taylor hummed while he considered my words. "What about you? Have you tried to start anything?"

I shook my head. "I've been going along with the status quo too."

"Well, maybe that's why he hasn't tried anything. Y'all need to sit down and have a chat or get sweaty. My vote is on the latter, but you do you, hun."

"You're right. I know you are."

"Mm-hmm. Now tell me everything. Spare no detail about Blond Ambition."

Over the next couple of hours I fulfilled Taylor's wishes while we chose our outfits and practiced our routine for the show. We were doing a duet tonight of Eve and Gwen Stefani's "Let Me Blow Ya Mind," and we wanted to stun. The moves were a lot sexier and coordinated than I was used to, but Taylor was exceptionally patient. He was a great teacher as well as a skilled dancer—especially in four-inch heels.

Mac had texted me earlier asking about my show tonight. I relayed the details to him, though I hadn't fully expected him to show up. As I peered into the main area of the bar from backstage, my breath caught in my throat when I spotted Mac at the bar. He looked exactly as he had the last time I saw him there: effortlessly sexy and good enough to take a bite out of. His Adam's apple bobbed as he swallowed a gulp of his drink—another fruity concoction—making me long for another taste of him.

Pull yer head outta yer arse, I told myself. Taylor was right in that I was just as responsible for the state of our relationship—for lack of a more apt word. Mac and I needed to talk. Perhaps it would be easier to broach the topic tonight after we'd both had a few scoops. *But look what happened last time you got drunk with him.* I wrinkled my nose at the thought, then left to go find Taylor.

"You good, sis?" he asked me with a wink.

I looked over at him, taking in his short, pink wig, red, plunging-V top, leather jacket, and white pants with black and red letters. He even had the fingerless gloves and fake paw print tattoos on his smooth, contoured chest. He looked stunning, and oh-so 2001. I was right there with him dressed in a yellow-and-blue-striped bikini top, red bomber jacket, and black pants. The ensemble was topped off with my blonde wig, black visor, and a gaudy, gold necklace that read "QUEEN." And I felt like one.

I nodded at Taylor then held up my fist, which he bumped with his own. When we walked out onstage and got into position, I spared Mac a quick glance, which he returned with a wink. The music started, and we put our well-rehearsed moves into practice. I felt Mac's heavy gaze on me the entire time, even when I had my back to him. I wanted to turn and seek him out, but I pushed the urge down and focused on not tripping over my or Taylor's feet. That would be just what I fuckin' needed.

We finished the routine without the whole thing going arseways at my hands, much to my relief. We went around schmoozing and collecting tips after, and I deliberately skipped over Mac. Taylor, however, did not. He leaned in close and whispered something in Mac's ear before he pulled a folded paper bill from in between Mac's middle and index fingers and walked toward me. Whatever he'd said left Mac wide-eyed and grinning.

"What was that about?" I asked him.

"I was just letting ya mans know he needs to use his pretty mouth for more than making you scream."

My jaw went slack and I blanched. "You're joking."

"Hunny, do I look like I'm playin' games right now? Y'all needed a push—consider this a shove," he replied with an eyebrow cocked.

"Puns are not appreciated right now," I mumbled.

He bumped his shoulder into mine and snorted a laugh. "Come, come. Let's get changed so you can talk to him."

I'd apologized to Mac when I met him at the bar. He was thoroughly tickled by Taylor's straightforward approach, though he agreed that Taylor was right. We went back to our flat to have some privacy with our long-overdue chat. I was a grimy, glittery mess, and opted to shower before we spoke. Mac was in the kitchen wiping down the counters when I finished. I took a seat at the island across from him.

"Do you want anything to drink?"

"Three fingers of Jameson would be brilliant."

"Wow, okay. I meant, like, water or juice, but we can have at the hard stuff." He brought out two mugs and the bottle.

"Tea mugs?"

"Mm-hmm." He held them both up on one hooked finger. "Handles make them easier to hold. And these are bigger than the fancy glasses." He poured God knows how much into each mug then passed me one. "Cheers."

"*Sláinte.*" We clinked mugs then I brought mine to my lips and swallowed down a liberal mouthful of whiskey. I shook my head and puffed my cheeks, releasing a deep breath.

"Where would you like to begin?" he asked without a hint of unease in his smooth, deep voice.

"Do you regret fucking me?"

"What?" He looked sincerely surprised by my question— a good sign. "Of course not. Do you regret it?"

I shook my head. "No. Why have you been acting strange?"

Mac's brows furrowed, and he cocked his head to the side like a confused puppy. "I haven't. Everything has been pretty normal."

"That's exactly what I mean. It's *too* normal. You're not freaking out at all, and you haven't…" I stopped myself before I could finish that pathetic, needy sentence.

"I haven't what?" He set his mug down with enough care for it to barely make a sound on the counter. He casually leaned toward me, gripping the edge of the counter and putting his sexy forearms on display. "I haven't tried to fuck you again? Is that it?"

I felt my face heat. I turned away from Mac before draining the contents in my mug.

"Yeah, that's what this is about," he drawled. "Dubhlainn, I left you alone because I wasn't sure you wanted me to touch you again. We had what I thought was a mind-blowing time, then you said you wanted to talk, which is fine. But you never talked to me. I figured you had a reason for putting it off, so I gave you space and respected what I thought was your decision."

Shite. This is my fault. "What about the rest of it? You're telling me you're just fine with what we did? With what that means for you?"

He shrugged. "I'm more than okay with the implications. I'm not torn up over not being able to call myself straight anymore. I already told you that I wasn't confused about what I wanted from you. That hasn't changed at all. In fact, I want you more now that I've had a taste. The only thing keeping me at bay is what *you* want. So, tell me: what is it you want, Dove?"

I chewed my bottom lip and regarded Mac carefully. How had I—*we*—let such an egregious miscommunication happen? "I'm so fuckin' dense," I muttered. "You are too. I was a dumbarse for putting off talking to you. When I saw how unaffected you seemed, I lost my nerve. I assumed you were pretending it never happened. And you"—I cut my eyes at him—"could have voiced your thoughts. We're both to blame for this awkward chinwag."

"I'm sorry, a what?"

"A chat, you arse."

"Ah." He bowed his head, though I saw the beginning of a smirk before he did. "Just to be clear, I'm going to ask you again: what do you want? If you tell me to fuck off, I will. But"—his voice dropped, sending a chill up my spine—"if you tell me you want this as much as I do, I can't be held responsible for what I do to you."

"Fuck."

"Yeah, I'd like to. Just say the word."

My cock stirred and started to stiffen. *Fuck, fuck, fuck!* "I…"

Mac moved around the counter, never taking his eyes off mine. He stood before me and lifted my chin up with his index finger. "I'll make this easy on you: yes or no?"

I nodded immediately.

"Nah. Say it," he pressed.

My lips parted and trembled. My entire body thrummed with the need to be touched—to be fucked. "Yes."

His hands were on me, drawing me against him, as soon as the word left my mouth. He kissed me with more pent-up need than a week had any right producing, and I returned his intensity. I slipped my fingers into his hair, and he did the same, tugging my head back. His tongue traced the pulse in my neck before he gently bit down on my collarbone. I sucked in a shaky breath and closed my eyes, letting the feel of Mac against me be my focus. He was hard in his shorts, his cock rubbing against my stomach.

He took a step forward and backed me against the edge of the counter, pushing aside the stool I'd just been sitting on. Strong hands grasped my ass and lifted me onto the counter. Mac forced my legs further apart with his larger frame, though I welcomed his heat. His lips crashed into mine in a bruising kiss, followed by his tongue tracing my bottom lip. I opened up to him and savored his taste while his sexy scruff tickled my jaw.

His kisses moved down to my jaw and neck, where he nipped my sensitive skin. "Arms up," he rasped against my neck. I lifted my arms and allowed him to pull my T-shirt off. His hands were back on me, though they moved slowly.

He traced my collarbone with his fingertips, then trailed feather-light caresses down the middle of my chest. I fought to remain still while Mac's fingers threatened to unravel me.

I opened my eyes and focused on his face. His jaw was clenched tight, accentuating his sharp jawline, and drawing attention to his kiss-swollen lips. His eyes followed the path his fingers traced along my chest. He appeared to be deep in concentration before his eyes suddenly met mine. *Why is he loo—*

A sharp intake of breath canceled all of my thoughts as Mac brushed his thumb over my left nipple. He did it again, though he had a smile on his face this time. His other hand rubbed along my stomach and hip, squeezing every so often. Mac's thumb circled the sensitive nub, then he pinched it, drawing a throaty moan out of me.

"Fuck yes," he hissed. He leaned in and flicked his hot tongue over my nipple a couple of times before alternating to slower, softer passes. I braced one hand behind me on the counter, and fisted the hair at the back of his head with the other. My cock ached and twitched every time Mac bit my nipple. When he moved over to the other one, my hips started moving in small circles. I was desperate for any friction on my cock, even if it only came from my pajama pants.

Lost to the pleasure from Mac's tongue, I missed that his hands had traveled down to the waistband of my pants. He flicked his eyes up at me without stopping his tongue's assault, and I knew what he was silently asking. I lifted my hips long enough for him to yank my pants down. Gravity took care of the rest and they fell from my dangling feet.

Mac pulled back from my chest and ran his hands from my knees to the tops of my thighs, brushing his thumbs along the crease on either side. "Fuck, dude. Do you ever wear underwear?"

"You're not in a position to lecture me over kex."

"Don't get me wrong—I think it's incredibly hot that you're free-ballin' it." His eyes dropped from mine and settled on my hard cock. I wanted to squirm under his stare, but I held my ground. Fucking me in the dark while we were drunk was one thing, but this was different. With the lights on and both of us—mostly—sober, there would be no getting around the fact that I was a man. That first time he kissed me and stroked my cock could even be ascribed to a momentary lapse, confusion, and general horniness. I knew it was a stretch, but I had to believe it was a possibility so that it wouldn't hurt when he came to his senses and decided he'd satisfied his fleeting curiosity.

I held my breath while I waited to see how this would go. Mac's normally carefree face looked so serious as he stared down at my now leaking cock.

Whatever lingering doubts I had about Mac shattered the moment he leaned in and closed his lips around the tip of my cock. I bit down hard on my knuckle to keep from making too much noise. I was usually able to keep myself under control, though that control crumbled whenever Mac was concerned.

Mac sucked harder on the tip, and I felt like I was going to bite through bone. He pulled off with a pop then pulled my hand away from my face. I opened my eyes to see him staring back at me while he leisurely stroked my cock.

"I want you to be loud. It's fucking hot, and I like knowing what's good for you."

My skin flushed, only in part due to my arousal. I felt it creep all the way to the top of my chest, burning me from the inside. Mac smirked at me then ducked his head down, guiding my cock back into his mouth. He took more of me this time, though he focused his attention on my cockhead, licking, sucking, and twirling his tongue. He went at it like he was eagerly sucking a lollipop for the first time and couldn't get enough. His actions were sloppy and unskilled without a sense of rhythm or any discernable pattern. Even so, his enthusiasm was almost too much. I was on the verge of coming after less than a minute. I'd be fuckin' scarlet if that happened.

I asked him to slow down, and he went faster. My cries of pleasure belied my words, and he knew it. The bastard. When my orgasm was within reach, I tried to warn Mac. He'd started massaging my arsehole, and my words got jumbled in my throat. Not giving him warning on his first time would have been a shite thing to do. On the edge and unable to think of anything else, I yanked his head back just as hot ribbons of cum shot from my cock, landing on his face and in his hair.

"I'm so fuckin' sorry," I panted. "I made a complete haymes of ya."

Mac cupped my balls then licked me root to tip, making me shiver due to oversensitivity. He swiped his thumb over the corner of his mouth, collecting the cum that had landed there. He pulled his hand back and regarded the mess before shocking me, and licking his thumb clean.

"You taste different than me."

"Pardon?"

"Your cum. It tastes different than mine," Mac clarified. "I'm not sure what I was expecting, but I like the way you taste."

His words made my skin break out in goose bumps. I looked away from him, perhaps more violently than necessary. "I'm not gonna thank you for sayin' that."

"I wouldn't expect you to." I could hear the amusement dripping from his voice and picture the cheeky smile on his handsome face.

A firm yank on my legs caught me off guard, and drew me to the edge of the counter. "What the hell are you—"

My words were cut off by Mac pushing my legs up toward my chest, and the scrape of his scruff on my most sensitive skin. His tongue made a slow pass over my arsehole, making me jump and gasp. Mac's strong arms wrapped under my legs and held me in place while his tongue worked me over, shocking me yet again. Mac alternated between probing with his tongue, light swipes, and nips to the surrounding skin. My cock stirred back to life like it was Easter fuckin' Sunday, then Mac pulled back, giving my sack a gentle nip along the way.

"I'm not done with you yet. Your room or mine?"

"Mine."

"Hang on." Mac scooped me up and held me against his chest. I wrapped my shaky legs around him, and kissed him, tugging on his bottom lip.

"I am fully capable of walking, you know."

"Shh. Kiss me, and stop acting like you don't love this."

I did as much, and rolled my hips, sliding my cock against his stomach. *Why is he still fully clothed?* I remedied that when we got to my room, ripping his shirt off before he set me down. I went for his belt while he backed me against the bed until the backs of my knees hit the mattress. Without a doubt, Mac was an alpha type of guy, inside the bedroom and out. He knew what he wanted and he had no issue taking it. I enjoyed that the first time we had sex, but I had other ideas now. I was *not* some ragdoll-twink he could just toss around and use—not all the time, at least.

I spun us around, and pushed him onto the bed. I told him to take off his pants then scoot up to the headboard, and smacked his hip when he took too long to move. He stared at me with wide eyes for a few moments before doing as instructed. I felt his gaze heavy on me as I moved to the nightstand and retrieved a condom and lube.

"What are you up to?" he asked with a cheeky playfulness in his voice.

I tossed the supplies next to him and shamelessly raked my eyes up and down his body. He was blond all over, and looked like a golden god sitting there with his eyes on me, stroking his thick cock. "You'll find out. Put that on," I said, nodding toward the condom.

Mac tore the package open with his teeth then skillfully rolled the condom down his length, giving the base a firm squeeze. "D'you want this?"

"Easy there, *dude*. Don't forget the lube."

Mac slicked up as I kneeled on the bed, never taking his eyes off mine. He looked at me like he was stalking his prey, though he was about to discover that this was my hunt. "Hands up. Hang onto the headboard and don't let go."

With an amused grin, he lifted his hands and gripped the headboard. I swung my leg over his hips so that I straddled him. His strong, thick thighs made it a bit of a stretch, but I managed. With my hands pawing at his chest, I rolled my hips and felt his cock slide against my arse. Unable to drag this out, I reached behind me and held him at the base while I slowly sank down onto his cock. It was easier with lube, but Mac was a hung bastard, and I couldn't escape the pain and burn of being stretched wide. I knew from experience that it would fade and focused on keeping my breathing steady to aid with that.

Mac tried to move a hand down, and I swatted him. "I told you not to move."

"Ow. You're a volatile kitty today," he replied, moving his hand back to the headboard.

I cocked an eyebrow at him and drew my nails hard down his chest, catching a nipple. He jerked involuntarily, driving his cock in deeper, making both of us gasp. I kept that momentum and began making small circles with my hips until I was stretched enough to fuck him like I wanted to. I kissed him while my hips continued their slow, tortuous pace. Mac whimpered into the kiss when I tweaked his nipples, which was a fuckin' deadly sound. To his credit, he kept still beneath me, even though I could tell he wanted nothing more than to flip me over and pound me into the mattress. His darkened eyes when I pulled back confirmed as much.

With one hand around the back of his neck and the other on his chest, I rolled my hips forward and back, faster and harder than before. Once I worked up a good rhythm, I leaned back and rested my hands on Mac's thighs for support while I moved. The new angle had his cock nailing my prostate, driving me crazy.

Several veins in Mac's forearms were visible as a result of how hard he was hanging on to the headboard. I hadn't expected him to last this long without moving, and wanted to show him my gratitude. I wildly bucked my hips, the sound of my cock slapping against my stomach momentarily drawing Mac's attention away from my face. As he stared at my cock I felt both self-conscious and even more turned on. He licked his lips, and that was it for me. I came hard, shooting all over his chest. My legs burned, and I felt like I was going to pass out from the overwhelming feeling of euphoria washing through me, but I kept moving until Mac's climax barreled through him about a minute later.

The muscles in his arms and abs flexed as he pulsed inside me, while his face held a look of concentration that morphed into bliss. With his cock still buried in my arse, I carefully sat forward and kissed him, twining my fingers around the back of his neck while my thumbs traced his jaw. I kissed along his cheek until I reached his lobe, which I teased with my tongue.

"You can move your arms now."

His arms instantly wrapped around me, pulling me flush against his chest. He buried his fingers in my hair, massaging my scalp, and gently tugging while he rubbed his cheek against mine. Our lips met, and the kiss was a flurry of tongues and heat that made my toes curl. No one had ever played with my hair the way Mac liked to, and I fuckin' loved it.

Mac drew back first. Huffed with a smile, and rested his forehead against mine. "Dude. Fuck. You totally just made me your little bitch."

A laugh rolled through me, making me wince when I realized Mac was still semi-hard inside me. I slowly lifted my hips, letting him slide free, before scooting a bit higher and lowering myself back down. "Aye, I did."

"Feel free to do it again any time. The whole no-touching thing was a bit painful, but you made it worthwhile."

Again. Right. "About doing this again—we need to have a chat about that." I rolled off of Mac and pulled the sheet up to my waist.

"Yeah, okay. Fun time's over." Mac looked down at his chest, running his thumb through some of my cum. "God-damn. You really messed me up today. Do you mind if I use your bathroom for a sec?"

"You do look a bit manky," I teased. "Go ahead."

Mac swatted my hip then got up. I watched his gorgeous arse as he walked into the jacks. When I realized he wasn't going to close the door, I turned away. I wanted to watch him, but I wasn't a fuckin' perv, and it felt wrong. He returned a minute or two later and hopped into bed, wiggling in under the sheet. I bit back a smile at his boyish nature.

"All right. I'll start. I'd like this to be a regular thing. Fucking you is even better than I dreamed it would be, and so long as we're both satisfied, I think we should keep this going."

I nodded, taking in his honest words. "I agree, though I need some rules."

"I'll adhere to whatever you say."

"Mm, so trusting. First, no marking me on my neck or anywhere else that's easily visible."

"But you like it. I know you do."

"Even so, if people see me with massive fuckin' hickies, there will be questions. That brings me to my second rule. Aoibheann cannot find out. I'm not asking to be your dirty little secret, and I won't treat you like mine, but a bit of discretion would be appreciated. Lastly, this arrangement is nonexclusive. I don't expect you to stop fucking around with women, and I don't want you to feel guilty for doing so."

Mac cocked an eyebrow at me. "And if I want to fuck other guys?"

My gut reaction told me to pin him and shout "no." The idea of Mac with other guys felt… wrong. I had no claim to the guy, but I hadn't considered that he might want to try out his newly uncovered sexuality with multiple partners. How foolish of me. "You're free to fuck whoever you want. As am I."

"Duly noted."

"Do you… want to sleep with other guys?" I hated that I asked the question, and how it made me sound.

He shrugged, then reached over and twirled my hair around his index finger. "I don't think so. I can't yet imagine walking up to a guy and asking him if he wants to fuck. That seems…" He sighed. "I don't know how it seems."

"You didn't seem to have any confidence issues when you kissed me and told me you wanted my arse."

Mac snorted a laugh and bowed his head. "That's totally

fair. So, how are we going to signal that we're good to go? Should I text you or just ask?"

"Really? A fuckin' text? Just come at me. If I don't want it, I'll let you know."

"Okay. You can do the same." His fingers in my hair stilled, and he worried his bottom lip. "Um, one last question. Were you serious before about the fisting comment?"

My mouth involuntarily went slack, and I gasped. "Absolutely no fisting! Unless it's my fist goin' up yer arse, you can forget about that shite idea."

His eyes went wide, and he yelped. He actually fuckin' yelped. "Fisting is off the table—forget I mentioned it."

"Good. Now get out of here so I can sleep. I'm knackered." I turned onto my side, and hugged my pillow to my chest. The bed dipped behind me, followed by Mac's lips on my shoulder, and his fingers stroking my hair. He wished me a goodnight, then left.

༄

I woke to the now familiar sound of Mac's music. It wasn't as loud as he normally had it, though it never was if I was still sleeping. I showered then went out to greet him, pleased to find a bowl filled with Froot Loops on the counter. Mac was sitting on the couch with his back to me, munching away on his breakfast. I added milk to my bowl then joined him on the couch.

He smiled wide at me, and we ate in a comfortable silence to the soundtrack of Mac's tacky rap music, and it was oddly enjoyable. As one song neared its end, Mac tapped away on his phone, then turned and grinned at me as "Luxurious" by Gwen Stefani started playing. I snorted and set my bowl down before I gave his arm a shove.

"Nice choice," I remarked.

"You think so? I'm trying to get in your pants, so I hoped it would work."

I lunged at him, climbing into his lap and kissing him fiercely. Mac wrapped his hands around me and flipped us, so I ended up flat on my back on the couch. He pinned me with his body while his mouth became intimately acquainted my mine, and every bit of skin he could reach. I closed my eyes and gave myself over to his touch.

He cupped my balls over my pants, and I pushed my hips into his palm for more. As he snaked his fingers under the waistband of my pants, I heard loud clicking on the floor, then felt something wet and cold on my cheek.

My eyes shot open as Eli's dog licked my face before going crazy on Mac's. Mac sat up, laughing and wiping off his face as the smile fell from mine. Prince wouldn't be here without Eli. I pushed Mac off of me and shot to my feet, straightening my clothes and adjusting my hard cock. Bryan stood in the entryway holding a plastic container and a black duffel bag. He grinned at me knowingly as Eli closed the door behind them. I faced Mac and hollered for him to turn the music down because we had company. He froze, suddenly seeming to realize what Prince's presence meant. He turned the music down then jumped over the back of the couch, meeting Bryan in a tight embrace.

"I'm sorry, dude. I didn't know you guys were coming by." He pulled back from Bryan and headed for Eli, pulling him into a hug and ruffling his short brown hair.

"I reminded you last night, though it seems you were a bit distracted," Bryan replied in an amused tone.

Eli stood close to him and held out a second plastic container. "Hello, Dubhlainn. We brought some cupcakes and macarons for you and Mac. Bryan made them last night."

I stepped forward and took the container from him,

thanking him. I took it over to the counter, along with the one Bryan held. I didn't know either of them well, though I had nothing but good views of either of them. I knew Eli through my sister. They've worked together for years, and are best mates. Eli has joined us on many holiday dinners over the years. He was a quiet guy, but once he met Bryan he started to open up. Bryan was, shite, Bryan was hot. Tall, dark, and handsome with pretty green eyes, a killer bod, and he knew how to cook.

I was surprised when I first met Mac after finding out he was Bryan's best mate. Aside from being stupidly attractive, they were quite different. Bryan was mature and sweet while Mac was… well, Mac. Now that I knew him better, I could see that the two would have balanced each other out.

I could see Eli eyeing me from the corner of my eye with a curious look on his face. He looked away and focused on Prince when I faced him, which I found odd. He did it again after I pretended to focus on the conversation Bryan and Mac were having. Weird—unless…

"Mac," I said, "do they know?"

That blond bastard shrugged. "They don't know everything."

"Somehow I don't believe you."

Mac had the audacity to look affronted. "Give me some credit. I didn't tell them how red you got last night when I tongue-punched your sexy boy bits."

Bryan burst into laughter while I was rendered silent due to shock. Eli looked between the three of us with his brow crinkled. "Tongue-punched," he murmured. When he clued in, he gasped. "Oh. *Oh.*"

Mac winked at Eli then puckered his lips at me. "You're just about the same shade of red right now, Dove."

I inhaled deeply, and was about to puck that bastard in the face, when Bryan stepped between us. "Easy, Dubhlainn.

I'm sorry I laughed. We won't tell anyone if that's what you want, and we're not here to judge you guys. You can murder Mac if you want to, but please let me take him to the game first. I'd really like to win, and we kind of need him for that."

I dropped my fist and stepped back, crossing my arms over my chest. "Fine. Take the gobshite with ya."

"Do you want to come watch the game?" Eli asked with a small grin.

I informed them that I had to work and politely declined. I thanked Eli and Bryan again for the baked sweets and excused myself to my room to get ready. When I was almost to my door, a hand far too gentle to be Mac's closed around my wrist. I turned back and was eye level with brown eyes that didn't belong to my flatmate.

Eli released my hand then tucked his in his pockets. "I'm sorry I grabbed you. I called after you, but you didn't stop."

"Sorry. I didn't hear you."

"It's okay. I just wanted to invite you to my birthday party. It's in two weeks. We're, um, going to go play laser tag then go out for some drinks and dancing." He took a deep breath and gave me a shaky smile.

While his anxiety had been getting better with Bryan, it was an ongoing battle for him that he might never fully overcome. I appreciated how difficult approaching me alone must have been for him and kindly accepted his invitation. I'd never played laser tag, and Eli was practically family. He gave me a smile that reached his eyes, and I caught a glimpse of what must drive Bryan crazy. He nodded then returned to Bryan and Mac.

Fuckin' Macalister. I'd kick his arse later.

NINE

MAC

I T'D BEEN NEARLY TWO WEEKS since Dove and I solidified our arrangement—and what a fantastic two weeks they'd been. Having great sex at my fingertips with someone as sexy as him was proving to be addictive. I wanted him constantly, and lucky for me, he was just as hungry for me. We got each other off every day, several times a day. He still cursed me under his breath if I tried to walk around the apartment naked, but I think he secretly liked it.

I hadn't realized it was possible, but my temperament had improved recently as well. I thought the guys on the team were going to kill me during our postgame drinks last weekend. I couldn't stop grinning, or shut up. Bryan kept his word and didn't tell anyone about my newly discovered interest in dick, though that didn't stop him from casting me knowing glances.

There wasn't particularly a reason for me not to tell the guys what was going on. Half of the damn team was gay, and they sure as hell wouldn't judge me. Axel would be shocked until he realized he had a better chance of getting girls when we went out. Maxim might just nod at me and carry on as if

I'd told him the weather. I'd known him long enough to know that very few things fazed that guy.

Not telling the team felt mildly dishonest, but I wanted to tell the rest of my family first. I was on my way over for dinner with Mom, Dad, and Miho, which would be the perfect opportunity to drop that bomb. We were having dinner a bit later than usual due to my work schedule. With Dove's ass always bouncing around in my mind and mere feet from me, I'd fallen behind with my work. I started getting up earlier and working later on the nights he was out to catch up. After working eleven hours straight today, I'd finally done just that. A few days of eye strain and a stiff back were small prices to pay for all the mind-blowing sex, in my opinion.

I parked behind Dad's car and left my doors unlocked. The house smelled like fragrant herbs and savory meat when I strolled in through the front door. *I guess we're having a roast dinner.* I announced my arrival and intercepted a hug from Miho on the way into the kitchen. Both of our parents were in there, working together to get supper plated and on the dining room table. I kissed my mom's cheek and clapped my dad on the shoulder.

"Mm, smells good in here." I leaned between them to get a better look at the food on the stovetop.

"Get out of here. Go wait with your sister and stop trying to pilfer food," Dad said to me.

I gasped. "You wound me, Dad. I would never."

"Honey, go away," Mom added sweetly with a pat to my cheek.

I backed toward the entryway to the dining room and pointed at my parents. "Just so you guys know, I am *not* feeling loved, and I'm totally going to tell Grams that you were mean to me." Their laughter faded as I turned and made my way over to the table next to Miho. "Are they like this with you too?"

"I know better than that. You don't get in the way when they're cooking. You should know this by now."

"Yeah, but I'm hungry. I haven't eaten much today."

"You're a grown-ass man, and that sounds like your own problem," she added with a smirk.

I rolled my eyes at her unwanted truthfulness. "Piss off, brat. Everyone in this family hates me."

"Don't be dramatic, Macalister," Mom said as she entered the room, plates in hand. "You're far too old for that."

"I can't win with you people," I whined.

Miho giggled while Dad came in with more plates. He leaned over and gave Mom a quick kiss before they sat down and uncorked a bottle of red wine. Not much had changed with them from when I was a kid. Dad's blond hair grew paler each year, though he was as handsome as he'd ever been. Mom's hair was always a darker shade, and still had no signs of graying.

We settled into our comfortable ritual of updating each other on our lives, and I gave updates on Bryan as well. My family had pretty much adopted him when he moved here from Texas back in university. He came from a big family, and we couldn't imagine him spending weekends and holidays alone. I'd all but dragged him home with me three days after we were assigned a dorm room together. He treated Miho like a princess, which solidified that he was a great dude in my mind. The rest of my family probably loved him as much as they loved me.

When chatter died down at the end of the meal, I took the opportunity to do what I came over to do. "I have something to tell you guys."

"Did you knock up some redhead? Oh my God, you did, didn't you?"

Grr. Miho.

Mom gasped, and her hand flew over her mouth. Dad sat quietly, watching me intently. "Honey, did you…"

"Hell no. Nobody is pregnant! Miho, shut it. Mom, calm down." I pinched the bridge of my nose and noticed Dad doing the same. "It's nothing like that." I took a deep breath, suddenly feeling nervous. This was my family. These people loved me no matter what, and I knew they wouldn't be anything but accepting of me. But it was still difficult to say. I'd already talked about it with Grams and Bryan, though it felt harder to say now. I swallowed a swig of wine, not commenting on the raised eyebrow Miho shot my way. "I think I'm bisexual."

Miho snorted a laugh while Mom and Dad looked at me with confused looks on their faces. Dad shook his head once at Miho, and she stopped laughing.

"Wait, you're being serious?" she asked.

"Yeah." My phone vibrated in my pocket, and while the distraction would have been nice, I ignored it.

Silence followed for a heavy ten seconds before Miho spoke again. "Are you sure?"

Her tone was so innocent that I had to laugh. "Yes. I'm not an expert, but I'm pretty sure I have enough empirical evidence to know I'm not exclusively straight." Miho wrinkled her nose at me, and I stuck my tongue out at her. The sound of throat clearing reminded me that we weren't alone, and my attention shot back to my parents. "Sorry, Mom. You didn't need to hear that."

"It's okay, honey. Your dad and I are well aware that you have sex."

"Unfortunately, I've seen it," Dad muttered under his breath, earning a whack on the arm from Mom.

"The point is, it doesn't matter *who* you're sleeping with. We just want you to be happy." Her kind smile made me feel all warm and fuzzy. The brief bout of nerves I'd had melted away, and my childhood home once again became a safe haven.

"What your mom said. You could have told us years ago and the answer would have been the same," Dad added.

Miho tugged on my earlobe, making me wince. "Yeah, why'd you wait so long to tell us?"

"I didn't know. This is brand new for me, and I'm still figuring some things out."

She nodded, mulling over my answer. "Have you ever made out with Bryan?"

"Ew, no," I lied. It had happened once.

Mom and Dad both sighed and stood up, disappearing into the kitchen with their dishes. I wanted to join them, but I'd have to face Miho's questions eventually. She went easy on me, not asking anything too invasive. We ended the talk with a hug, and she even kissed my cheek and told me she was happy for me. Mom and Dad came back in, we had dessert, then I headed out.

In my car, I checked my phone and saw a message from Rebecca, an old hookup I hadn't seen or heard from in months. She was free tonight and asking if I wanted to drop by. Before I knew what I was doing, I was thumbing out a message to Dove, asking if he was going to be around tonight. Our agreement stated we weren't exclusive, yet I hadn't slept with anyone else in the last two weeks. He was always my first choice—trying for anyone else hadn't even occurred to me.

Dove replied back saying he was out with Taylor and would be late. Good enough. I messaged Rebecca to forward me her address, then drove off toward West Town with a feeling in my gut that I could almost equate to guilt.

⊙⊙⊙

THIS IS THE END. I was pinned down and surrounded by three enemy combatants: Bryan, Maxim, and Axel. I'd managed to tag Eli, Eve, Samir, and Dove, but there's no surprise there. From my position behind an overturned table, I was at a severe disadvantage. If I moved, I'd maybe take down one of them before getting shot. Maxim's aim was the least accurate of the remaining three, though he'd be compensating for that by hanging back with his weapon aimed and ready. Axel was the fastest, and Bryan was the best shot and had the most experience. Bry also had the best chance of predicting my next move.

"Come on out, *rubito*," Axel teased from my right. "You're only prolonging the inevitable."

"Eat me!" I yelled back.

Bryan snorted a laugh from my left. He sounded close—closer than I thought. "Let him strategize. This will be over in a minute or two."

Eve and Dove took turns launching teasing words at me, clearly bitter that I'd taken them out early. No matter. Their taunts wouldn't distract me from my victory. I'd go after Axel first—take him out, and use him for cover against Bryan and Maxim. I had to wait for the right moment to strike, or I'd be tagged as soon as I surfaced. Eve said something delightfully vile that no proper lady had any business saying, causing the others, including Axel, to laugh.

I used that distraction to roll out from behind the table, tagging a stunned Axel as I rose to my feet. His vest changed colors from green to red, and he let himself drop, cursing in Spanish. Anticipating this, I moved in and caught him, pulling his limp body against me. I took aim at Maxim, and tagged him, then scanned my left for Bryan. *Where the fuck is he?*

"Behind you," my best friend purred before he shot me in the back.

I dropped Axel then fell to my knees in a dramatic display before I collapsed on top of his much smaller frame.

"*Pendejo!* You weigh a ton." Axel shoved at me until I took pity on him and rolled off.

Everyone came over to congratulate Bryan on his victory and rib me for coming so close then losing. Once I was on my feet, Bryan playfully slapped my cheek then pulled me into a tight hug. "You baited me into thinking you were on the left."

The guy shamelessly smiled and nodded. "You took the bait, just like I knew you would."

"Dude, playing against you is so unfair."

Maxim walked over and nodded his head at me as he passed, which was the closest to a "well done" I was going to get from him. The man saved his words like they were kittens in trees. That was the last of five games we played before packing up and heading out for a sushi dinner. We met up with Blake and Santiago at the restaurant, then said goodbye to Eve and Samir after the meal.

We ended up at a popular gay bar for drinks and dancing about an hour later. I bought the first round of shots and toasted the birthday boy, who shied away from the attention with flushed cheeks. I threw back my shot then ruffled his hair and grinned at him. "Happy birthday, Eli. You're going to have to let me plan something huge for your dirty-thirty next year."

"Oh, God," Bryan whined, while Eli laughed and shook his head.

"I'm thinking Vegas."

"I'm not going to Vegas with you again," Bryan replied. "You couldn't pay me."

Eli's brow crinkled, and he looked between me and Bryan. "What happened in Vegas?"

"Nothing," we both answered in unison. Bryan leaned into Eli and said, "I'll tell you later."

Yes, please tell your fiancé about that time we got drunk and ended up making out in a hot tub so I could be the meat in a showgirls sandwich. Not. I couldn't plead without drawing attention to myself, so I left it alone for now, turning back to the bar for another drink.

Drink in hand, I scanned the dance floor for some familiar faces and found Blake's golden-blonde hair. She was dancing pressed up against Axel, and the kid looked like he was in heaven. She was altogether too much woman for him, but that didn't stop him from trying. Blake and I briefly dated, then did the friends-with-benefits thing for a few years until we discovered that we were more like siblings. She was a tall, leggy blonde in every sense, with piercing blue eyes, and a sharp tongue. Axe-Man wasn't ready.

Santiago was dancing with a lively black-haired twink a few feet from Axel and Blake. I could tell he was just being polite, and that the guy's advances were in vain. Santiago didn't go for twinks—they reminded him too much of his students, which gave him the "heebie-jeebies," as he so fondly put it.

To my surprise, I spotted Dove talking to Maxim—and Maxim was actually smiling. Wide. I shouldn't have been surprised. The kid was amusing and gorgeous, and not even Maxim could remain stoic in front of that. I was glad to see Dove getting along with my friends, even if I was a wee bit jealous that it wasn't me he was talking to. With his ripped jeans, worn band tee, and hair up in a messy bun, he looked like a sexy rock star.

Deliciously indecent thoughts flooded my mind, reminding me of all that smooth, pale skin under his fitted clothes. My feet moved of their own accord and led me toward Dove. I only made it a few steps before coming to a halt in front of the petit strawberry-blonde who'd placed herself in my path. She flashed me a pearly white smile, wrapped her arms around my neck, and swayed with the music.

By the end of the third song, she—Ellie—was basically dry-humping my leg. She smelled like coconut, and her curves felt so good under my hands. Her green eyes kept me in a trance until she asked me for a drink. I skipped off to the bar and ordered two vodka sodas and a shot. Bryan slid in next to me while I was waiting.

"I see you're getting pretty cozy with that girl," he said.

"Her name is Ellie, and she likes dancing and my firm ass."

He rolled his eyes at me. "Dubhlainn is watching you."

I looked over my shoulder and found Dove and Maxim still talking, though Dove had his arms crossed now. He didn't look angry otherwise, and why would he be? We'd made it clear that we could sleep with other people. I turned back to Bryan with a shrug. "And?"

"And? Really? This is going to get messy, Mac."

The bartender returned with my drinks, and I slung back the shot. I set down the glass, cupped Bryan's shoulder, and winked at him. "Everything will be fine, Dad."

TEN

DUBHLAINN

I HAD NO RIGHT TO BE JEALOUS or upset. I had no fuckin' right, yet there I was, all but puffing green smoke as I watched Mac chat and dance with a woman. She'd marched up to him, thrown her arms around him, and laid her claim. Had she done it to anyone else, I'd have applauded her confidence. Instead, I contemplated going over there and inserting myself between them. But to what end? If I made a holy show out of things, I'd only ruin my arrangement with Mac—and that was too good to pass up. To make things worse, she had to be a fuckin' gingernut.

I tried to focus on Maxim. He didn't say much, but he managed enough to keep a conversation going. Despite his minimal speaking, he remained engaged and focused on me when I spoke. I couldn't quite figure out what his deal was. The guy was massive and hot as hell, so I wouldn't think he had confidence issues. Several men and women came around, vying for his attention, and he politely rejected each of them.

His brown eyes were darker than Mac's, almost so that they appeared black in the dim lighting. *Mac.* I chanced another glance his way and saw that floozie plastered to him.

The tips of my ears burned with misplaced rage. She hadn't done anything wrong, and neither had Mac. The only person who'd fucked up in this scenario was me, and that made me angrier.

"Macalister isn't very smart when he isn't in someone else's business."

My eyes darted back to Maxim, and my mouth fell open in surprise. "Sorry?"

"Macalister." Maxim motioned to him with his head. "He talks a lot, and surprisingly gives great advice, but he's blind when it comes to his own affairs."

I narrowed my eyes at him, not wanting to give anything away. "What are you trying to say?"

"The others might not have noticed it, but I've seen how you two look at each other. You've been unable to focus since he started dancing with that redhead."

I opened my mouth to protest then shut it when Maxim cut his eyes at me. "Sorry."

He shrugged. "It's okay. You should go talk to him."

Mac caught my attention again. His hands were on her hips, moving up to cup one of her breasts. *Fucking hell.* I was about to tell Maxim he was wrong about the whole thing, but he was no longer standing before me. I did a full three-sixty looking for him, but he was gone. How a man his size managed to slip away would have been impressive if not for my shite mood.

Standing around watching Mac wasn't accomplishing a thing. I had to do something. Perhaps finding someone of my own would distract me. The club was packed with viable candidates, several of which flashed me interested smiles and fuck-me eyes as I passed by. I wanted to find the right guy, and I knew I'd know him when I saw him.

After ordering another drink with my fake ID, I scanned the dance floor, skimming over the nameless and faceless bodies, settling on Mac. Again. He was saying something in his partner's ear, and she was smiling. My fingers tightened around my glass, and I wanted to throw it—at a wall, at her, but mostly at him. I drowned the rest of the whiskey, and turned for the bar, slamming into a wall.

"Are you okay?" a deep voice asked.

I looked up to see that the wall was in fact a *very* handsome blond with pale blue eyes, and a dimpled smile. The guy was built like a linebacker. "I'm fine, thank you." My eyes scanned him from head to toe, enjoying every last bit of him.

"I guess you're all right if your priority is to check me out." He smirked, accentuating his dimples and making him even more attractive.

I held my head up high and looked him in the eye. "I like what I see. Can you blame me?"

"I suppose not." He held his hand out, and smiled wider. "Name's Jason."

Jason and I had a few drinks and became *quite* acquainted while we danced. As much as I was enjoying his company, in his arms wasn't where I'd wanted to be. No matter how hard I tried to ignore him, my attention kept drifting over to Mac. Only this time when I looked over, I was shocked to see him staring back. His gaze was heavy on me, while his hands were all over her. He continued to watch me on and off, and I was helpless to look away.

Blake and Axel came around a bit later to tell me everyone else was heading out. Mac appeared at her side with his little gingernut, and she repeated what she'd just told me. They hugged and quickly pecked on the lips before separating.

"I think we're going to head out too," he said, eyeing his date.

I more or less declared the same thing, grabbing Jason's hand. Mac's eyes dropped to my hand in Jason's, and he scowled before sniffing and schooling his expression. He wasn't acting like himself, but I supposed it was likely the alcohol.

Blake's gaze shifted between me and Mac. "Perfect timing! You guys can split a cab."

I wanted to scream "no," though Jason's deep voice, and the floozie's high one, cut me off. They apparently thought it was a brilliant idea.

What a fuckin' holy show. I found myself in a taxi on the way back to the flat, with not only Jason, but Mac *and* his floozie. Jason was the tallest and sat in the front while I leaned against the passenger-side window, trying to make myself as small as possible in hopes I'd disappear. I should have known that lady luck wouldn't have sided with me. Mac sat next to me, though he was too preoccupied to notice I was there, let alone that I was fuming.

The hellish ride ended, and I bolted from the car, forgetting all about Jason. He called out for me, halting my retreat. When I turned around to go back, I bumped into Mac and reflexively gasped when his brown eyes found mine and he smiled.

"Slow down, kid." He reached for me but stopped with his hand in midair. He glanced over at my date and shoved his hand into his pocket. "You should go get your guy." His tone was cold, and so unlike him. Mac wrapped his arm around his date's shoulders, stepped around me, and headed inside.

What the hell was that? I couldn't worry about him right now. With all the energy I could muster, I turned a seductive smile toward Jason and welcomed him to join me inside.

No polite small talk occurred once we all got inside the

flat. Mac had taken hold of his date's hand and swept her off into his room, slamming the door behind them. When we were alone, Jason stepped in close and laid his claim on me with a scorching kiss that would have made my toes curl, if not for the fact that I wished he was someone else.

I led him down the hall to my room, though I knew I should have just sent him home and gone to bed. We started slow with kissing and his exploratory hands on me. He asked me what I liked, and I was about to reply when a high-pitched moan crept into my room. My head snapped toward the shared wall with Mac's room, and I cursed the eejit who built the place and skimped on soundproofing. She moaned again, longer this time, fraying my will to be a responsible, logical adult.

Jason was oblivious to my inner turmoil and stood waiting for my answer to his question. "I want you to throw me against that wall then fuck me until I can't stand."

"And here I was, trying to be a gentleman," he quipped.

I unbuttoned my jeans, and pushed them down, trying not to flinch with every new sound coming from Mac's room. "I don't want a gentleman tonight."

He scooped me up, backed me into the shared wall—not as hard as I'd hoped. Not like when Mac threw me around. Jason bit my neck, causing me to throw my head back against the wall and groan. There was a pause from the other room before the sounds started back up, louder than before. I bit Jason's collarbone harder than I should have. He gritted his teeth and hissed instead of crying out as I'd hoped. It was petty and childish, but I wanted to one-up Mac for every sound I heard.

Jason pulled me from the wall, and carried me over to my bed, dropping me down. He whipped his shirt off then stroked his fingers over the fresh bite marks I'd left on him.

"I'm trying to go easy on you, man. I don't want to hurt you."

He was too nice. I felt like an arsehole for using him, but I couldn't stop now. "It's fine. I'm not going to break." *At least not physically.*

❀

IN ALL THE chaos of last night I'd left my curtains open. The sick, empty feeling in my stomach woke me from a restless sleep, while the blinding sun ensured that I'd actually have to get my sorry arse out of bed. It was early—earlier than Mac usually got up on the weekend—and I didn't hear any sounds from Mac's room or the kitchen. Satisfied that I could move about without having to face him, I got up, threw on a shirt and some sleep pants, and went to the kitchen.

Mac was nowhere to be found, thankfully. I drank a glass of water, and was in the middle of refilling it when the front door opened. I spun around and leaned back to see around the corner, stunned when Mac stepped into view. He had his gym bag with him and was breathing hard.

I turned away from him before I wished him good morning, distracting myself by running the tap. I heard his bag hit the floor followed by footsteps until I could feel the heat radiating off of him from directly behind me.

"What the hell was up with last night?" he asked me in a clipped tone.

I cocked my head to the side, turning around with a scowl. "Excuse me?"

"All that banging against the wall and porn star moaning. You put on quite the performance."

"As if you have any room to judge me. You're the one who started it."

He snorted, though it wasn't in amusement. "So I wasn't

mistaken in feeling like last night was a contest. Had I known you wanted to play games, I'd have turned out all by best tricks."

"Fuck you," I ground out.

"Sure you're not too tired to after last night?" He flinched after the words left his mouth. "I'm sorry. That was uncalled for. I just don't get what's going on."

I crossed my arms and shrugged. "You had a pretty good grasp of the situation last night with what's-her-name."

"Oh, so you can fuck other people, but I can't?"

"That isn't what I'm sayin'—"

"Why is that suddenly a problem?" he pressed on.

It struck me then that I hadn't had an issue with the other times I'd known Mac had slept with other people. He'd come home smelling like sex or with hickies, and I never had a problem with it. But seeing him with that woman, and then having him bring her home—

Ah, that's it. I hadn't had to see it before. Mac had never brought women home in the time I'd lived with him, even before we started fucking. Why had he done so last night? Why did I even care? Even if I didn't know why I was jealous, the fact that I was remained. How did I expect to explain that to him, when I couldn't make sense of it to myself?

I sighed, releasing most of the fight in me. "It's not a problem."

He scoffed. "Clearly it is."

"*This* is exactly why I was hesitant to do this with you. Why are we even fuckin' havin' this fight?! This was a mistake." I pushed past him toward the hall, but he grabbed my wrist, stopping me. I turned toward him with my fist clenched, ready to puck him in the jaw. I deflated and unclenched my fist when I saw his face. With a heavy sigh, he cast his eyes down and looked like a dejected puppy.

"Just wait a minute." He let go of me then ran his hand

through his hair. "I didn't mean to come at you this morning. Well, that's not true. I wanted to, but I knew I didn't have any right to. I was going to pretend last night didn't happen, and move on… then I saw you when I got in, and I couldn't stop myself from coming over and being a dick."

Uh, what the fuck? "Sorry, what're ya sayin'?"

Mac's jaw clenched then he nodded to himself, like he'd been debating whether to tell me or not. "I got insanely jealous last night when I saw you dancing with that guy." My eyes widened in shock. Those were not the words I'd been expecting. "I know it's hypocritical and stupid." He shrugged. "It doesn't change how I felt. Seeing him with his hands all over you pissed me off. I brought that girl here last night to rile you up after you'd said you were bringing your guy back. I'm sorry. I really didn't know I was such a possessive asshole."

I huffed, my shoulders slumping forward. Mac deserved honesty from me. "I felt the same. I only picked up that guy after I saw you dancing. Part of me wanted a distraction, but there's a big part of me that hoped you'd be jealous. My foolishness only made things worse by the sound of it."

He snorted a laugh. "Is that so? Shit. We're doing great at this uncomplicated, fuck-buddies thing."

An unexpected laugh bubbled up, easing some of the tension between us. "Shut your gob. How do we fix this? Add in a new rule about not bringing people back here? And maybe no fucking around at mutual friends' parties," I added dryly.

"No. That's too much work. You're hotter than she was, anyway." My eyes went wide again. Mac had just said I was hot. *Wow.* "Why are you looking at me like that?"

"You said I was hot."

"Um, yeah. Of course you are. It's not like I haven't said it a thousand times already—don't derail the conversation."

"You haven't said it before."

It was his turn to be taken aback. "Really? Jeez, I am an asshole," he muttered. "Look, I think you're a smoke-show. I'm sorry I didn't tell you before. Frankly speaking, I'd rather keep this thing going with you than sleep with other people. We get along and have great sexual chemistry. If it's cool with you, I'm fine with altering the arrangement."

"Altering it how?"

"Casual, yet exclusive. No fucking other people. No more drama."

"Exclusive friends with benefits. Deadly idea—that'll work for me. Are you sure it's what you want?"

Mac nodded immediately. "Absolutely. Like I said, it works with you. We've both got a possessive streak, and this takes care of that without messing things up. I'd have proposed it sooner had I known something like last night could happen."

I winced and nodded. "Sorry about that."

"It's fine." He waved his hand between us while he spoke. "That's over and done."

"That guy was a fine thing, but he wasn't as good as you, anyway," I teased.

Mac's mood shifted. His brown eyes conveyed mischief and fire, and his lips curved into a grin. "That 'fine thing' was huge and worked you over pretty good by the sound of it. I'll give you today off before I remind you just how much better I am. That, and I need to buy more condoms today."

"What if we stopped using them?" The words were out of my mouth before I could stop them.

Mac raised an eyebrow at me. "Explain."

"If we're not going to fuck other people, we can consider getting tested and ditching condoms altogether. We don't have to, it just came out."

He hummed, considering it for only a few seconds before

turning a wide smile on me. "I like it. I can only imagine how much better it's going to feel to—what's the term? 'Breed that bussy.'"

Hearing those words out loud was worse than cringey. I found myself cursing Mac in my granny's native tongue before I could think twice about it. "*Imeacht go fánach ort féin is ar do chnapán miúlach!* Do not *ever* say that again."

"I don't know what you just said, but I'm going to assume it was bad. Yeah, I feel like I need a shower now after saying that." He shook his shoulders and shivered.

"You're far too vanilla to stick that kind of dirty talk," I muttered.

"Excuse me? I am *not* vanilla. That's essentially calling me a basic-bitch at sex." He actually sounded affronted. It was fuckin' grand. He pulled me into his arms, telling me all the filthy things he'd do to me, and I couldn't help but find the whole situation gas. My laughter only made his protestations worse, which made me laugh harder. He ended up kissing me and giving me a blowjob to shut me up. It worked.

ELEVEN

MAC

DAYS LATER, AND DOVE's blow still stung. Me—vanilla? The nerve of that kid. I was in serious need of reassurance—and cookies—so there was no better place for me than Grams's apartment. She'd actually agreed with Dubhlainn, though I found sympathy and support from Mrs. Baker and the other sweet ladies at the complex. I'd spent the day playing games, eating freshly baked goods, and fixing up anything that required "the touch of a strapping young man," or so I'd been told. I knew that there was a fully capable handyman on staff, just as those sweet ladies knew that I'd enjoy spending time with, and being useful to, them.

Miho hadn't been so kind at our family's Fourth of July barbecue. Before dinner, I'd pulled her aside and quietly asked her if she thought I was vanilla. Her response was to burst into laughter and take off to go tell Mom what I'd asked. The two of them cried from laughing so hard at my expense. Dad and Grams were having a hushed conversation in the living room, so at least they weren't there to join in on the ribbing at my expense.

I'd managed to convince Grams to come over for the day,

which was a great feat considering she wasn't fond of traveling much these days. We always went to her for holidays and visits, but I really wanted her at the house this year, at least once. Christmas or Thanksgiving would have been preferred because they felt more like family holidays, but the weather would have made traveling harder on Grams, and I wanted her trip to go as smoothly as possible.

We ended up having a marvelous time, with only minor teasing between me and Miho. I brought a ton of leftovers home to share with Dove and was delighted to see he'd brought back two containers full of food from his visit with his sister and her husband. Dove was in the shower, so I took the containers out and had a little peek. One was some kind of beefy, brothy, potatoy, carroty thing. The visual wasn't so great, but it smelled good. The other dish was a feast for the eyes and nose. I think it was lamb over rice with some type of yogurt-based sauce. I scanned the counter and released a throaty groan when I spotted a bag of what appeared to be fresh, homemade pita bread. Surely, Dove wouldn't notice if I had one little taste.

In hindsight, I probably should have left the food alone. Dove came down the hall just in time to catch me stuffing my face with the last chunk of the single pita I'd taken out of the bag. He cursed me black and blue, though his tone held no vitriol. I could see his lips trembling, trying to hold back a smile. Seeking his forgiveness, I dropped down to my knees before him and asked what I could do to make amends. The flush that spread over his pale skin was almost as lovely as the shade of his beautiful hair.

I'd been enjoying making him blush every day in the nearly two weeks since Eli's birthday. As discussed, we'd gone and gotten tested for every STD under the sun and were awaiting the results. Neither of us wanted to spend money on condoms after Dove's supply ran out, so we'd taken to getting each other off by more creative—but no less enjoyable—means. I felt like I was sixteen again and just discovering how fucking amazing sex was.

°°°

I'D BE LYING if I said I hadn't been distracted. Fooling around with Dove had been perfection, but in the back of my mind, I hadn't forgotten about Dove's vanilla comment. I had every intention of proving him wrong. I'd make him swallow those words—I was just biding my time until I figured out how.

One scorching July afternoon, I'd finally figured out *how* I'd prove it. It was ungodly hot, and our baseball game had just ended in a damn tie. Postgame drinks were going to be a shit show, though I had other ideas. Any time I had a problem, if I didn't ask my family—which I was *not* doing this time—I'd ask my friends. Bryan was immediately ruled out. If I was vanilla, he was basic vanilla to my French vanilla. I loved the dude, but asking him for kinky advice would have been pointless. Axel was too young and inexperienced. Santiago might have been into some wild shit, though we weren't quite at that stage where I wouldn't feel weird asking him. Blake would have made fun of me to no end, which I wasn't remotely in the mood for. Which left Maxim—why I hadn't thought of him first was beyond me. I chalked it up to a blond moment.

Maxim was very private in all aspects of his life, but I'd been around him longer than the other guys. I knew him back when he had a serious boyfriend, and I was unlucky enough to stumble upon them in the middle of some wild fuckery involving a spreader bar and rope—or so I'd been told. I'd promised Maxim not to speak of what I saw, and he promptly took back the emergency key he'd given me to his place. Apparently, running out of milk hadn't been an appropriate emergency to use the key.

I strolled over to Maxim while he was packing up his gear and casually leaned against a fence post, pretending to take in the sights of the park and its patrons. Maxim finished packing his bag before he spared me a questioning glance, which I returned with a cheeky grin.

After another minute or two, he broke. "What is it you're after?"

My composure broke, and I sank down onto the bench next to his bag. "Ugh. I thought you'd never ask. I need your help with some shopping today."

"No."

"You didn't even ask what kind."

"It doesn't matter."

I leaned in closer, lowering my voice when I asked, "What if I told you it involves what I saw back in college? You know, that fateful day I ran out of milk and came over."

Maxim narrowed his eyes at me, as if trying to make sense of my words—then it struck him. His eyes widened with realization, and his jaw clenched. "You promised me, Macalister."

"And I intend to keep that promise. I'm not trying to blackmail you or anything." I stood up and stepped closer. "I'm out of my depth, and I need some help, dude."

He was silent for long enough that I thought he wouldn't reply before he sighed, rubbing the back of his neck. "Is this about Dubhlainn?"

"Wh—no. What are you talking about?"

"Don't lie. You were never any good at it," he replied dryly.

"Okay, fine. Yes, it's about him." I went on to explain what Dove had said, and how soul-crushing it was to hear. Maxim scoffed and told me to go easy on the hyperbole, but he agreed to accompany me on a very brief shopping trip.

I stopped myself from jumping for joy to avoid drawing attention to us and instead held out my arms wide. "Yaas. Bring it in, big guy."

"No."

"Yes."

"No."

"Maaaxy—"

"I'll hug you if you promise not to call me that again."

I hauled him into my embrace, patting his shoulder. "Atta boy. I know you're just a big softie, even if you play tough and stoic." I released him and ruffled his brown hair, making him blush. His head whipped around us, probably making sure no one saw. "It's okay. No one is looking."

He nodded, taking a step back from me and slinging his bag over his shoulder. How someone as handsome and cool as Maxim had confidence issues, I'd never understand. He had a small scar on his upper lip that he was insecure about, but people found that sexy. It was very Joaquin Phoenix and only added to his rugged good looks.

I told him I'd go tell the guys we wouldn't be joining them, which he thanked me for. The guy was an introverted teddy bear under his hulking exterior. He'd put up a fuss over the hug because we were in public, but I knew Maxim liked being tactile with those close to him, even if he liked to pretend he didn't. Seeing him try to keep his collected composure in a sex shop was going to be fun.

༄

"Do you have any more crisps?"

"Any more what?" I replied.

Dove sighed in frustration. "*Chips.*" He said it with so

much damn sass that I couldn't help but laugh as I handed him another bag. "Thank you. These aren't chips, and they never will be."

"Whatever you say." I fluffed the pillow behind me then leaned back into it, cushioning my back from the headboard of my bed. When Dove got home I'd invited him for some Netflix and chill in my room. I hadn't literally meant it, but he looked so happy at the prospect, and I couldn't put a damper on that. So, there we sat, leaning against the headboard of my bed, watching *Space Jam*, and eating junk food in our underwear. It was kind of perfect.

I had a few surprises for him under my pillow from my earlier outing with Maxim, as well as mail from the clinic where we were tested. I waited until the movie ended to make my move, pulling Dove into my lap, facing me. I nipped the tip of his nose, and grinned at him, unable to contain my excitement for what was coming.

"Stop actin' the maggot—you look ridiculous right now."

"I don't know what that means, but I'm not going to stop being happy."

One corner of Dove's mouth quirked up. "What are you up to?"

I reached behind me, grabbing the envelopes, and presented them to the fiery sprite in my lap. A small gasp fell from his lips, and his eyes shot to mine. "Are those the results?"

"Mm-hmm. Want to open them? If you'd prefer privacy, I can close my eyes."

He snatched the envelope addressed to him, then punched me half-heartedly in the chest. "Arsehole." He tore into the letter, and I did the same. "Negative."

I turned my results around, showing a clean bill of health.

"I have another surprise." I snatched up the papers,

tossing them on the floor, then flipped us over. With Dove on his back looking up at me with a playful smirk, I reached under the pillow and pulled out some padded black leather cuffs.

"Thoughts on being tied up? I'll make it worth your while?"

Dove raked his teeth over his bottom lip, causing it to flush with color. He studied the cuffs in my hand before turning his attention to me and nodding. Heat pooled in the pit of my stomach as a wide smile stretched my lips. *I'll show you who's vanilla.*

I kissed each of Dove's wrists before fastening his hands in each padded cuff. Once his hands were bound, I felt under the pillow for the thin chain I'd hooked to the metal frame under the bed earlier. Once I felt the other end, I pushed Dove's hands over his head, and hooked them to the chain behind the pillow. He tested his restraints with a few good tugs, one corner of his mouth quirked in a devious smile.

"What do ya plan on doin' to me?"

Hearing his accent come out thicker had my cock twitching with need. I went a little crazy at the store and had *so* much planned. "I'm gonna make you sweat," I said with a wink, reaching for my phone on the nightstand.

"Tell me you're not quoting that awful song you listen to."

Oh, but I was. I hit play on the Spotify playlist I'd prepared, and the room flooded with the opening saxophone riff of "Careless Whisper."

Dove's eyes widened, and he shook his head. "Change the mus—"

I pressed my finger to his lips, silencing him. "Shush." I leaned down and kissed him, tweaking his nipple with one hand and retrieving another surprise with the other. I stroked my thumb against the soft feather in my hand. I'd seen it earlier and just about died at the thought of using a feather to tickle and tease Dove. Maxim had sighed and shook his head, but I thought it was the best damn thing.

I kissed Dove's neck, enjoying the feel of his body writhing at my mercy and the soft moans he was making. Deciding he was ready for more, I angled the feather toward Dove, stroking him from his armpit, down the side of his ribs. He instantly flinched, pulling away from me as much as his restraints would allow.

"What the fuck was that?"

"Don't worry about it. Stop moving." I drew the feather down the middle of his chest, gently tickling his skin. Dove started protesting again, and I pressed my lips to his, quieting him. "Shh, just let it happen." I twisted the feather over his nipple, which turned out to be an awful idea.

"Mac, get the fuck off me *right now*."

Uh-oh. I unfastened his wrists then sat back on my haunches with a nervous grin. Dove scowled at me as he pulled the sheet up to his neck. *Well, shit. This isn't how I imagined this going.*

"What the fuck was that?" he repeated.

"Um, a feather." I held up the offending plume.

Dove's scowl deepened. "I know it's a fuckin' feather. Why did you think that was a good idea?"

I sighed, my shoulders slumping. "I don't know. I wanted to prove that I wasn't boring and vanilla. I guess that was an epic fail, huh?"

The anger bled out of his features, replaced by what almost looked like sympathy. "I said you were vanilla, not boring." He punched me in the chest then flicked the tip of my nose. "And I didn't say there was anything wrong with that. Dumbarse."

I cringed, wanting to bury my head under the pillows. "Can we just forget that this happened?"

Dove snorted a laugh, shaking his head. "Ya haven't got a snowball's chance in hell of that happenin'."

"Was it really that bad?"

"I could have forgiven George Michael, but that feather was too much. The cuffs were fuckin' class. We can use those again—without the other shite. Come 'ere."

I crawled up his body until my face hovered a few inches from his. Dropping my head into the crook of his neck, I exhaled deeply. "I'm sorry."

"Yeah, I know. Don't get all twisted up." He planted a quick kiss on my lips then winked at me. "Do you want to watch another flick? I don't have a TV in my room, and this is rather grand."

I flopped onto my back, and handed him the controller to my Xbox. "You pick one. I'll go get more chips." I rolled out of bed, heading for the door but was stopped by Dove's voice.

"If ya stop moping about I'll give you an Aussie kiss when you get back."

Well, that put a smile on my face.

TWELVE

DUBHLAINN

I woke late for a Saturday morning. A colleague had asked me to switch shifts, resulting in me working a double until midnight last night. Mac was bumping around in the kitchen, his cheesy, endearing music thumping through the flat. I used the jacks, washed my face, then strolled out to the kitchen.

I sucked in a breath at the sight of his round, bare arse swaying side to side in tune to the music. The only stitch of clothing on him was a charcoal-gray apron; the ties were knotted low on his back, the ends dangling over the globes of his glorious arse. He flashed me a smile brighter than the sun when he noticed my presence.

"Good morning," he said cheerfully—too cheerfully for how knackered I felt.

"Mornin'." I rubbed my eyes then did a double take at Mac. "Wait, are you cooking? Something other than bacon?"

He shrugged. "I can make pancakes. My grandpa taught me his famous recipe when I was a kid." He made a show of jerking the nonstick pan, flipping the pancake.

I snorted a laugh, shaking my head at his antics. "Why are you making pancakes?"

"That's a stupid question, but you're sexy as fuck, so I'll allow it." He winked at me, and I rolled my eyes. "First, pancakes are the shit, dude. That, and Bryan brought over a fuck-ton of blueberries from the bakery last night. One of the new employees accidentally doubled the order. Second, I feel a little guilty over last night, and this is me trying to appease you." His smile turned shy, almost boyish.

Heat rushed to my cheeks and neck at the fresh memory. I'd been dead on my feet when I got home, exhausted after working a double shift. Mac had rushed out of his room, literally scooping me up in the dark. He took me back to his room, stripped me bare, and fucked me into the mattress—hard. He'd held me in a bruising grip, and had bit and slapped my ass hard enough to leave marks. It was one of the hottest things ever done to me. I faintly remember him kissing me and carrying me to my room afterward.

"If you think you did anything that deserves an apology, you're gravely mistaken."

"Have you looked at your ass in a mirror yet?"

"No."

"Then please don't do so until I'm out of punching range."

Giggling—I hated that he made me giggle—I took a seat at the island, watching him cook and dance. He took a seat next to me once he'd made enough pancakes for two generous stacks. He asked me about my plans for the day, nodding silently when I answered that I had none. The quiet stretched on between us, feeling oddly uncomfortable. I was about to ask him what he was thinking about when he spoke up.

"Do you think you might want to come with me to visit Grams today?"

My eyebrows scrunched together at his awkward delivery. Was Mac nervous asking me? One look at him told me he was. He was unsettled, scratching at the corner of his plate with one hand and tracing his fingers over the blond hair on his thigh with the other. Okay, so he was nervous. Why was he inviting me at all? Whatever the reason, with the way he anxiously looked at me, there wasn't a single part of me that wanted to decline. "I absolutely would. Your granny sounds fierce."

The relieved smile that overtook his features had me leaning over, pulling him by the apron straps into a searing kiss. A distant voice inside my head warned me to not get too comfortable with Mac. He was my flatmate and my fuck buddy. He was affectionate by nature, but me kissing him— even having the urge to do so—outside of sex was dangerous. Mac was the kind of addictive that could get me in trouble if I wasn't careful. He was the kind of man who could destroy me if I let him.

⸰°⸰

"YOU BROUGHT A FRIEND WITH YOU." Mac's granny turned from him to me, extending her hand. "And what a handsome young man you are."

I smiled and took hold of her hand, bringing her fingers to my lips for a kiss. "You flatter me. It's a pleasure to meet you. I'm Dubhlainn Ó Donnghaile."

"Wow, so proper and fancy," Mac teased.

"Fuck off, will ya." I froze, eyes darting to Mac's granny. "I'm sorry for my language. My granny would have my head if she heard me effin' and blindin' in front of a proper lady."

Her eyebrow cocked, and her lips curled into a grin—the same one as her grandson. "That's quite all right, Dubhlainn. If one of these proper ladies you speak of appears, I'll be sure to send her out on her proper ass. I'm Mac's grandmother. Please call me Daisy."

I stared at her for too long. Mrs. Buchanan was a beautiful woman oozing an air of confidence. Her silver hair was fashioned in a neat bun, and she was dressed in a coral fitted lace-overlay dress and cardigan, with nude block-heel pumps. "Jaysus, are those Manolo Blahniks?"

Mac leaned into her, whispering, "Didn't I tell you he was the cutest thing?"

They shared a laugh at my expense. I was scarlet, though I managed a smile. "All right, let's move this along farther into the apartment before we make a scene, and I get hauled away to taste test five different types of cookies. You know, on second thought." Mac made for the doorway, stopping when his granny reached up and grabbed his ear. "For God's sake, Grams, I was kidding."

She pulled him back then pushed him farther into the apartment, cutting her eyes at him. She flashed a kind smile at me and invited me inside, apologizing for her "foolish" grandson's antics. Over the next hour, we became better acquainted over easy conversation and cribbage. Daisy wasn't at all like my granny, but being around her, and seeing how much Mac loved her, filled me with a bittersweet feeling. On one hand, I was grateful to have been included in this cherished family time, yet it reminded me of how much I missed my granny. My granny was a sweet woman who always made sure you were warm and fed. If I fell and hurt myself, it would be her to pick me up and tell me I was stronger for surviving. She spoiled me with love, much like I could tell Daisy did with Mac. She seemed to have a blunt, teasing relationship with him, but the immense love was clearly there.

Throughout the game, Mac updated Daisy on his week, often looking to me and asking questions to include me. He conveniently left out all the sex we'd been having, for which I was thankful. Daisy asked me about my degree and growing up in Ireland before she told us of the few times she'd been lucky enough to visit Ireland and Scotland. By the time she and I finished our stories, Mac vowed to never travel to either place due to the local cuisine. Ireland's version of black pudding and Scotland's haggis had made his face contort in a particularly amusing way.

A knock at the door had Mac darting away from the culinary discussion faster than I'd seen him move for anything else—except maybe sex. He greeted a woman he addressed as Mrs. Ashburn, who apologized for intruding. She told him that her oven's light bulb had burnt out, and asked him if he could change it for her before he went home today. Without missing a beat, he agreed to help and hollered back to Daisy and me that he'd be back shortly. As soon as the door closed, she smiled, turning her full attention on me.

"How old are you, Dubhlainn?"

"Nineteen."

She stood, making her way over to a mahogany cabinet in the corner. "Would you like a drink? You'd be old enough at home, and that's all I need to keep my conscience clear." She turned back to me expectantly.

"Yes, please. Whatever you're having will be great."

She grinned, her brown eyes sparkling. "Good boy." She pulled down two tumblers, filling them halfway with clear liquid before returning to the table. "I take it Mac drove you two over today. I figured you and I could indulge a bit."

I took the glass she held out for me, suppressing the memory of riding in Mac's death trap he'd called a car, then clinked mine to hers. "*Sláinte*," we said in unison. I lifted the glass to my lips, nearly gagging when the herbal taste of gin hit my tongue.

"Not a gin man?"

"I wasn't expecting it. I haven't had much gin." I took another sip, handling it much better.

Daisy hummed in amusement, tapping the side of her glass. "He likes you."

I reasoned she had to be talking about Mac. "I like him too. He's a decent flatmate."

She cocked her head at me, narrowing her eyes. "That's not what I meant, and I know you're not that thick. Mac told me about the two of you." Her tone was neutral, cordial even, as she eyed me knowingly.

I lifted my chin, refusing to squirm in my chair under her intense gaze—the same one Mac used on me. "He did say you two were close. What makes you think Mac—"

"No, dear. I don't think he likes you—I know he does."

I shook my head. "No, I don't think he does. That's not what our rela—arrangement is about."

"How long have you lived with him?"

"Around two and a half months."

"I've known Macalister for his entire life. I held him in my arms minutes after he was born. I know him better than he knows himself, Dubhlainn. When I listen to him speak of you, and today when I've seen how he's looked at you, it's clear to me that he cares deeply for you. His voice is filled with so much adoration when he tells me about you. He told me he thought you were beautiful."

Beautiful. Jaysus fuck. "Oh."

"You haven't noticed it?" she pressed.

I thought about her words only for a moment. If I let myself, I'd easily get lost in my head, over-analyzing every interaction with Mac. Doing so would end up with me over-complicating our uncomplicated arrangement, which was not what I wanted. "Mac has treated me the same since day one."

Daisy raised a critical brow at me and sipped her gin.

"Okay, not exactly the same. Things have obviously changed some." I downed the rest of my gin to distract myself from shifting uncomfortably. Talking about sex didn't bother me—even if it was with the granny of the guy I was fucking. Talking about Mac and me meant thinking more what this whole thing meant to me, and that was dangerous. Mac was a great guy and far too easy to get along with. He was kind, giving, so devastatingly handsome that it hurt, and —*stop. Just stop.*

I cracked my neck then met Daisy's stare. "I care for him, but it's not what you think it is." *It can't be.*

She nodded, her critical expression unyielding—she didn't believe me. "I won't pry any further, dear. It was not my intention to make you uncomfortable."

"I'm not uncomfortable."

The corners of her lips lifted. "Be careful with him. I don't want to see either of you hurt."

I nodded, flashing her a grave smile. I didn't want that either.

⚬⚬⚬

THE SHIFT from hell was nearing its end. I'd spent the entire afternoon fucking up one task after another, causing even more work for myself. Right before my lunch break I knocked over a display of canned soup and had to sort through them, taking out the dented ones, before setting it back up. A salad dressing sample station was my next victim, followed by a twenty-four-pack of Coke. Three cans had broken. After I mopped up the mess, my manager had pulled me aside and chided me. I hated being talked to like an incompetent eejit, but I was sure acting like one.

My latest fuck-up happened after my manager had left. I'd knocked over all of the cereal boxes on the pallet in front of me and half of the ones on the shelf while I'd been scrambling. All of those missteps because I couldn't focus on my fuckin' job. I couldn't focus on anything other than Mac.

Why had his granny said those things? As much as I tried, I couldn't push thoughts of him aside. Just this morning he'd had breakfast laid out on the counter waiting for me; nothing fancy, just Froot Loops poured into a bowl with a spoon already in it and a glass of orange juice in the fridge. The warm smile he'd greeted me with, followed by the gentle yet demanding kiss he'd stolen when I sat down was everything. Seeing the boxes of Froot Loops on the shelf had sucked me back into that memory. I'd leaned against the stacked pallet, toppling over its boxes and knocking over the ones on the shelves as I fell.

Get a fuckin' grip, Dubhlainn. I tidied up the mess, saying a prayer that all of the boxes were salvageable. It'd started spittin' down on my last break, and I wasn't looking forward to getting soaked to the bone while I waited for the bus. I could leg it. I'd get wet either way, though my army boots weren't great for running.

Fifteen minutes before my shift ended, my phone vibrated in my pocket. With no one else around, I pulled it out, unlocking the screen with my fingerprint. A text from Mac had my brows climbing high. He didn't ever text me when he knew I was at work.

M: I'm here to pick you up, kiddo.

M: You're off soon, right?

M: Oh no. Dude, is this the day when you work super late???

I stifled a laugh, shaking my head.

D: I'm off at seven. I'll be out in ten.

M: Thank God.

Ten minutes later, I was running out toward Mac's death trap—never happier to see the thing. He'd come to pick me up. I still had trouble wrapping my head around it. I'd never asked before, nor had he offered. So why now?

"Thank you for picking me up," I said quietly, closing the door behind me.

"Of course. I'd just finished up with Bryan at the gym and noticed it was pouring. We wouldn't want you getting swept away in the rain." He winked at me, his lips lifting into a smirk.

I wanted to roll my eyes or shake my head—brush him off as I usually did—but I couldn't. I sat there, just staring at him, warring with myself over how to proceed. Mac's amused expression turned serious, and he captured my chin between his finger and thumb.

"Are you okay, Dove?"

I managed a nod then shrugged. "I had a long day."

Mac flashed me a sympathetic smile while he slid his hand around my head to play with my hair. It felt so good that I let my eyes flutter closed. They shot open again when his soft lips pressed against mine in a short, sweet kiss.

"Sorry you had a shitty day. Bryan baked us a cake. I can pick up some pizza or something for supper if you don't feel like cooking." His fingers continued stroking and twirling around my hair.

Was this normal? Very little about Mac was. I knew he was an affectionate person, but this felt so much more intimate than what we'd previously shared. Perhaps I was reading too much into things, searching for validation in Daisy's words. "That sounds brilliant."

He smiled and kissed me again, nipping my bottom lip before pulling back. "I can think of a few other things I can try to cheer you up with when we get home." He kissed my jaw and down my neck. His soft lips and tongue perfectly contrasted his coarse stubble on my sensitive skin. I melted under his touch. I wanted everything he'd give me, whether my mind told me it was smart or not.

⚬[⚬]⚬

A FEW DAYS LATER, I was met with another invitation from Mac: this time for a family dinner on Thursday evening. I'd said yes without hesitation when he'd cast that nervous expression on me again. He could have asked for anything when he made that face.

"You're going to like it," he said, leaning over me at the counter, his hands firmly on my waist and arse, drawing me into him. His lips were inches from mine, getting closer. A knock at the door interrupted, and he pulled back with a groan of frustration. "This had better be important," he muttered, stomping over to the door.

I grabbed my phone off the counter, wincing when I saw a missed call from my sister last night. I hadn't seen her in a couple of weeks and had been pretty shite at replying to her texts in a timely fashion. I was about to call her when Mac's surprised gasp caught my attention.

"What the fuck are you doing here?" he asked with clear happiness in his voice. He stepped aside, and a beautiful Asian girl around my age strolled inside. Her eyes instantly settled on my near-naked form, making me cross my arms self-consciously. *This is what I get for listening to Mac and waltzing around in my kex.*

"I was in the area visiting Blake—"

"You would still visit my ex."

"Shut up. She's cooler than you."

"Yeah, you're right." Mac closed the door then turned his attention on me. "I'm being rude as hell. Dubhlainn, this is my kid sister, Miho. Miho, this is Dubhlainn—my new roomie."

She strode up to me with a big smile and held her hand out. "I haven't heard enough about you. My dear brother failed to mention that you were a total babe."

Jaysus, they're just alike. I snorted a laugh and shook her hand. "You flatter me."

Miho gasped. "You're Irish? Like, actually Irish? That's so cool."

Mac appeared behind her, picking her up in a bear hug, and walked her several feet from me before setting her down by the couch. "Down, girl."

"Why are you so extra?" she snapped at him.

"Why are you so thirsty?"

They bickered back and forth like a couple of children while I looked on with a grin. They might not look alike, but the two siblings were very much the same.

"Why do you constantly have to cock-block me?"

"It's not gonna happen, sis."

"Oh, don't 'sis' me."

"Sure thing, kiddo," Mac replied dryly.

"Oh, you—" Miho jumped on her brother, smacking him and protesting that she was not a kid. Fuck. I probably looked just like that when I protested.

"Give it up. You can't win. Besides, it's not gonna happen with him," Mac repeated.

She cast a narrowed gaze on Mac before realization crept into her features. *Interesting.* Miho pulled out her phone, fingers typing away. Seconds later, Mac's phone beeped from the couch where he'd left it. He ignored it, only going to retrieve it at Miho's insistence. I leaned back against the counter, watching the two madly text and make accusing eyes at each other. I let them go on for a full minute before dropping my arms and groaning.

"You two can speak openly. I'm not a fuckin' eejit."

Their fingers stopped at that. Miho looked up and pointed at Mac, then me. "You guys are totally fucking."

Mac cringed. I remained silent, curious to see how he'd handle this. "Dammit, Miho."

She shrugged. "He said to speak openly."

Mac looked to me, a silent question in his eyes. I nodded once. "Yes, we're fucking," he said to Miho.

"Is it serious?" She bounded over to her brother, voice rising with clear excitement.

"It's not like that. We're—" Mac looked to me, his eyes pleading for me to interject. I shrugged, tipping my head toward him to continue. "We're casual."

"Casual as in taking things slow or…"

"We aren't dating," I said, pushing off of the counter. I headed toward the table by the bay windows, where Mac had stripped me of my T-shirt. I whipped it over my head, relaxing a bit at being covered. I still didn't have any fuckin' pants on, but I'd left those in my room.

"What he said." Mac motioned toward me with his thumb.

Miho pranced over to me and took hold of my wrists. "I have a million questions for you. Did Mac make the first move or—"

"Chill, sis. It's early, and we were kind of busy. Now skedaddle, and you can play twenty questions over supper on Thursday." Mac pried her hands off of me. I bit back a grin, finding the events of this morning both amusing and strange.

"So, you've invited your not-boyfriend—whom you're sleeping with—to our family barbecue, *and* you expect me to 'chill'? That's not going to happen, brother." Miho's hands went to her slim hips, one finger tapping.

"I invited my friend and roommate to supper, which is totally fine. Now leave."

"Make me," she teased.

I'm surrounded by children.

"Fine. Stay as long as you like." Mac's hands skimming my waist and arse startled me. My attention quickly turned to Miho, watching us with wide eyes. "If you insist on being here while we continue what you interrupted, you're going to get quite an eyeful." In an instant, Mac's lips were on my neck, and his body was firmly pressed against mine, my back to his front. He tore at my clothes and touched me like we were alone. I had to bite my cheek to keep from moaning.

"Fuck, okay, okay. I'm going." Miho's heels clicked as her long strides took her to the door. She opened it, then turned back. "Nice meeting you, Dubhlainn—see you at supper."

I didn't get a chance to respond before the door closed and she was gone.

THIRTEEN

MAC

I COULDN'T TELL YOU WHY I was so nervous to have Dove meet my parents, but I was. I'd brought friends over for supper before, and it was no big deal. Bringing home someone I was sleeping with—even if we weren't dating—felt like a huge deal. I hadn't done it since Blake. She and I weren't serious and were under no illusions that we had anything close to love. My poor parents had been hopeful it would turn into more. I learned my lesson after we stopped sleeping together and my family still wanted to see and hear from her. It was fine in that case since we remained great friends, though I wasn't confident that would always be the case.

My situation with Dove wasn't exactly the same. He and I sleeping together was—kind of—a secret, and we'd agreed that it's just sex. We weren't going out on dates and being each other's plus-one to events like Blake and I had done. Things with Dove were even more casual, yet somehow so much more. It could have been our decision to ditch condoms, or maybe just that I liked hanging out with him as much as I liked fucking him—well, almost as much. He was my friend; above anything else, I was happy to say that we were friends now.

So why was I so nervous?

"This is a beautiful house," Dove said, glancing around the spacious entryway of my parents' home.

"I'll pass that on to Mom and Dad."

"They're not here?"

I sniffed the air, catching a whiff of Dad's secret barbecue sauce marinade. "Nah. The car wasn't in the driveway, and knowing Dad, he forgot something for supper. Mom would have gone with him to make sure he didn't forget again." A thought sprouted in my mind for how we could pass the time. "Do you want a tour? We can start with my bedroom."

He rolled his blue eyes at me, his lips lifting in a grin. "Smooth."

"Yeah, but I know you want to see it." I didn't give Dove a chance to be snarky or obstinate. Taking his wrist in hand, I led him up the stairs, and around the bannister, to my bedroom door. "Brace yourself. I wasn't always as cool as I am now."

"You? Cool? I must have missed that memo."

I flicked his ear then opened the door and led him inside. Motioning around my old room, I said, "Behold the wonders of my youth."

"It was so long ago, I'm genuinely surprised you remember."

"I'm going to spank you if you keep acting like a brat," I said with a grin.

"Does that mean I should start calling you Daddy now?" he asked with a raised brow.

"Sure thing, sport."

Dove's face twisted, and he shook his head. "Wow. Never call me 'sport' again. That's got to be the least sexy thing I've ever heard."

I hopped onto my bed, bracing my arms behind me for support. "I'm vanilla as fuck, dude. Have you forgotten? And I don't think daddy kink is for me. I'll try it if you want to, but I can't promise I'll be any good at it." I'd called him sport for fuck's sake—I doubted daddy kink was in my future.

A smile pulled at Dove's lips, and he shook his head. "That's quite all right. Vanilla is my favorite flavor, anyway." He turned from me, taking in my trophies and posters.

"Close the door," I instructed.

He did so without question, whistling when he caught sight of the massive Jean Grey poster on the back of the door. "Jaysus—you're a closet nerd."

"Um, have you seen her? She's gorgeous. Smart, powerful, hot as hell—Jean Grey is the complete package."

Dove was quiet for a moment, looking over the poster from top to bottom. "What came first—your love for her or your interest in coppertops?"

I stood up and walked over to Dove, wrapping my arms around his waist and drawing him against me. "She was first. I'd be lying if I said she wasn't why I like redheads so much." His hair was tied back, allowing me easy access to his neck. I kissed his exposed skin, slowly grinding my hips against his ass. I tried to slip a hand under his shirt, but he stopped me. I ceased my advances, dropping my hands to my sides. "What's wrong?"

Dove chewed his bottom lip, staring off toward the posters above my bed. I said his name, catching his attention. "Sorry. I was thinking."

"About what?"

I didn't get his answer. My mom's voice called out my name, and Dove's mouth snapped closed. He was quick to spin around and open the door, leaving me alone in my room. *Weird.* My dad's voice hollered for me next, asking if I was here. *Best not to keep them waiting.*

Whatever happened with Dove in my room was forgotten when we got downstairs. I introduced him to my parents, who were very excited to meet my new roommate. Miho walked in after them, a smile turning up the corners of her mouth when she laid eyes on Dove. She hugged him then hauled him off to the living room to chat. I helped my parents in the kitchen, periodically checking to make sure Miho wasn't asking Dove anything inappropriate. To my amusement, they seemed to be getting along a bit too well. I stopped popping in on them after I overheard Miho telling Dove about how sexy the guys in Prague were.

"Why don't you go sit with your sister and…" Mom started.

"Dubhlainn."

"Yes, thank you."

I huffed, taking a seat on a kitchen stool at the counter. "Are you trying to get rid of me? I promise I won't try to steal any food."

"You don't cook, son," Dad added with a smile.

"I can still sit here and watch. Miho and Dubhlainn are getting along. I want to leave them alone for a bit longer." For whatever reason, it was important to me that they liked each other. My parents glanced at each other, doing that nonverbal communication thing longtime couples were so good at.

"Okay, dear. You can stay in here for now. But please don't touch anything." Mom patted my hand before scurrying off to the fridge.

"Yeah, yeah, I'm a disaster in the kitchen—I get it."

"You can't be perfect at everything," Dad quipped. We shared a laugh, and he asked me about work, and I did the same. My father was considering retiring soon, but he didn't want to leave his company behind yet. I broke his heart a little by not following in his footsteps and becoming an architect, though he respected the career I chose because it made me happy.

Supper was a huge success in every respect. Dad's ribs and Mom's potato and egg salad were fucking amazing, and everyone liked Dove. He was a bit nervous initially, but that quickly melted away. My parents weren't uptight, intimidating people, and treated him like family.

I spent most of the night watching Dove interact with my family seamlessly. Dad engaged him over castles and cathedrals in Ireland, while Mom was more interested in hearing about his family. Miho refrained from outing him at the table and kept her questions geared toward pop culture and all the mutual interests they'd uncovered. It felt like Dove had always been there, and that made me feel really damn good.

THE NEXT NIGHT, I watched in awe as Dove performed to No Doubt's "Simple Kind of Life." His bright pink wig of teased curls was in stark contrast to the white wedding dress he wore. Halfway through the performance, he pulled an orange and red flower bouquet out from under his dress. When he'd initially come out, I was expecting a kickass punk performance. Then the music started, and he slipped into character. The conflict and pain on his face had me wholly focused on his every movement, disregarding everyone else in the bar.

I shuffled the party popper Dove had given me before he went backstage to get ready. He'd handed out several, and gave me instructions to pop mine at the three minute mark when the lights changed. I did as instructed, as did everyone else with a popper, and the room was showered in white confetti. It was snow in July in the beautifully melancholic scene before my eyes. It wasn't your typical drag show, though it was mesmerizing all the same.

Dove was on his knees when the song came to an end. Raucous applause and whistles filled the room, which he graciously stood to accept. I couldn't bring myself to clap. If I moved I faced the possibility of sliding off my stool, and taking him into my arms. This was only an act, yet I couldn't quell the desire coursing through me to comfort him. He was smiling while he collected his tips, but it wasn't enough—*I* wanted to make him smile. I was desperate for it.

When he came around to me, his brows drew together as concern bled into his beautiful face. He was halfway through asking me if I was all right when I grabbed him. I hauled him close to me, crashing my lips to his in a brutal kiss. The desperation coursing through me dimmed enough for me to answer when he asked me again if I was all right.

"I'm better now."

Dove glanced around the bar then back to me. "Wanna go back to the flat? We don't have to linger around here tonight."

I nodded my head and bit my bottom lip to keep from kissing him again.

"I'll be right back. I just need to grab my stuff." Dove disappeared through the crowd, and the urge to be near him was nearly suffocating. Was this my jealousy again? It felt different—stronger. I turned to the bar, grabbing my forgotten drink and draining the glass. The taste of the watered-down cocktail made me wrinkle my nose. I wasn't acting like myself, and more alcohol probably wasn't the best idea. Going home and being alone with Dove was probably the best course of action until I got a handle on myself.

Dove hadn't even changed before we left the bar. When we got home, he unpinned his wig in the living room, set it carefully on the table, then turned toward me near the door. "What's going on with you tonight?"

"I don't know. I think I'm just tired." Dove didn't look convinced, but he didn't call me out. "You were stunning tonight."

He grinned, his eyes lighting up. "So you like the dress then?" He tipped his head back, beckoning me to have a taste.

"Yeah, I do. I'd like it a lot better around your ankles."

He kicked up one leg, setting his foot on the coffee table. "Come get me."

I managed one step before his voice halted me.

"On your hands and knees."

Without hesitating, I dropped to my knees, and crawled over to him. By the time I reached him, my cock was rock-hard in my shorts and begging for any type of friction. I couldn't recall a time where I'd ever been more turned on by someone fully clothed. Glancing up at Dove, I wrapped my fingers around his ankle up on the table, and under the dress around his other thigh. My fingers easily glided over the white thigh-high stockings he wore until both hands connected with skin. His legs were unshaven, and as hot as the stockings were, I preferred the feel of *him* against my palms.

With heavy-lidded eyes, Dove looked down at me and stroked his fingers along my jaw. "Still tired?"

I grabbed his wrist, holding it in place while I kissed the tips of his index and middle fingers. "Not a chance. Take the dress off."

Dove brought his raised foot down to the floor. He unzipped the side of the gown and let it drop, standing before me in only stockings and white lace briefs that were clearly designed for men, given the pouch barely containing his hard cock.

"Fucking hell," I scraped out, brushing my thumb over the wet spot at his tip. He shuddered, fisting his hands in my hair, urging me on. I brushed my cheeks over the bulge in his briefs before gently nipping at him. "Get on the couch."

Dove swallowed hard, then stepped around me and sat down on the couch with his legs spread. I crawled over to him and pulled off his briefs, stuffing them in my pocket—because I was a fucking panty thief now. Wrapping my hands under his thighs, I pulled him to the edge of the couch, going straight for his hole. I wanted to take him hard, and I wanted to ensure that he'd be ready for it.

He writhed as my tongue lapped over his hole, penetrating the tight muscle every few swipes. Giving head was still a weak spot for me—though Dove always got off on my sloppy technique—but I took to rimming right away. Lucky for me, Dove loved either. I could make him come from just eating him out, and on another day I would. Letting go of his right thigh, I felt around between the cushions until I found the bottle of lube we'd stashed there weeks ago.

Since the decision to be exclusive, we discovered it was a great idea to have lube *everywhere*. The freedom to have at each other whenever and wherever we wanted was thrilling; I was in a near-constant state of arousal for him. I knew what he liked, and I knew what he could take. He never asked me to stop or slow down because he didn't have to. The thought of being buried inside him made my cock twitch, still confined in my shorts.

With one hand, I popped the cap on the lube, and flipped it upside down, dribbling a generous amount in my palm. I replaced my tongue with two slick fingers, opening Dove up, and stroking his prostate. Dove's back arched, and his moans almost had me coming undone. I wasn't going to last once I was inside him, so I wanted to do everything I could to get him close. I bent down and closed my lips around his pink cockhead, swirling my tongue against the sensitive underside. From there I sucked and licked him wildly. My problem was that I couldn't focus on just one technique, so I did everything. Dove liked to rag on me for it, but I had him close to coming after less than a minute with my mouth and fingers. I pulled back and withdrew my fingers, going to unbutton my pants.

"No, don't stop," Dove sighed.

I kissed the inside of his knee while I slicked up my cock, shuddering at the contact. His eyes locked with mine as I lined up my cock and pressed into him, sinking into that exquisite tight heat, inch by inch. Once my balls pressed against his ass, I pushed his legs back, gripping under his bent knees. I pulled almost all the way out then watched my cock disappear inside him on my next thrust. Picking up speed, I rolled my hips into him, gritting my teeth at the sensation. As good as it felt, I needed more.

I pulled out on the next thrust, Dove's protests once again reaching my ears. "Hang on to me," I said harshly, out of breath. Dove hooked his ankles around my back and slung his arms around my neck before I picked him up and walked us over to the closest wall. Knowing he didn't mind it rough, I slammed Dove into the wall then worked my arms under his knees to hold him up. I drove back into him hard and fast, causing him to inhale sharply.

"Hang on, babe. This is gonna be rough."

Dove's eyes widened then he nodded, hanging on to my shoulder and neck. I snapped my hips up into him with so much force that our neighbors probably heard my skin slapping his. I fucked him relentlessly, each thrust pushing me closer to blowing. Taking more of Dove's weight, I pulled him away from the wall so only his shoulders leaned against it. The new angle had me nailing his prostate with every drive into him.

His lips parted on a moan before the biggest smile overtook his face. He pulled me closer and kissed me, and I felt a wave of relief rush through me. I lost track of time—of everything except the feel of him in my arms, around my cock, and against my lips. All of my senses were dominated by him, and I'd never felt more alive.

He came first, biting down on my neck and whimpering as I fucked him through it. My orgasm nearly brought me to my knees seconds later. I pushed him back up against the wall for support and clung to him, not ready to let him go. My cock remained inside him while we leaned against each other, panting and gasping.

"Jaysus fuck." He cupped my cheek with one hand then kissed me. "Do you feel better now?"

"I don't like seeing you sad," I admitted.

His head cocked back and his brows furrowed. "When was I sad?"

"At the club. Sitting there on the floor… you looked so heartbroken. It got to me, I guess. I don't know." I looked away, though I made my attempts to put him down or move.

"Hey. Look at me. That wasn't real. This…" He shook his head, swallowing hard. "I'm all right. I promise. Don't go all quiet on me again. You freaked me out."

"My bad. I don't know what came over me. I just wanted to make you smile."

He flashed me a shy grin as a flush colored his cheeks that had nothing to do with how good I'd just fucked him. "Put me down. You can't hold me up forever."

I scoffed. "I bet I could. You're like a buck thirty soaking wet."

"There it is—now you're back to normal. Arsehole."

"I think half of that might be from your gorgeous hair," I said, slowly pulling out and setting him down.

He mumbled something under his breath as he headed down the hall, stopping at the shared bathroom and flicking on the light. "Join me for a shower if you want to put your estimate to the test." He disappeared inside the bathroom, and the sound of the shower spray reached my ears seconds later.

My feet were moving before my brain could catch up. *That* was an opportunity I wasn't going to miss.

FOURTEEN

DUBHLAINN

*T*HIS IS REAL. I'd nearly slipped and said that to Mac the other night. What a fuckin' disaster that would have been. The fact that those words had been so close to spilling out had me reeling—even two days later. I didn't have to question where they came from because I knew. As soon as they'd almost been spoken, I knew they were true for me. I didn't know exactly when I fell for him, but I had.

This is real. It was very fuckin' real to me, and that was a problem. Mac and I had agreed to keep our relationship casual, and I'd fucked that up. I should have known this would happen, or at least caught on sooner, and put a stop to us sleeping together. I should have done *something*.

But I didn't. I let myself fall, and now I didn't know what to do about it. Well, I knew that I should end things, but the selfish bastard in me liked Mac and didn't want to. Fretting about it in bed wouldn't solve any of my problems. As much as I didn't want to tell her, I needed to talk to Aoibheann. If luck was on my side, she'd be able to give me some perspective—or at least calm me down.

I got up, pleased to find a bowl of Froot Loops waiting

for me on the counter. To my surprise Mac was dressed—fully dressed—and at his computer. The smile he flashed my way made my insides twist with a mixture of guilt and happiness. I managed to return the gesture, and asked him why he was dressed while I busied myself making tea.

"I'm going to see Grams today. You wanna come again? She liked you, but I guess you're pretty likable," he said with a wink.

"Maybe next time. I was hoping to catch my sister today."

He stood, scooping up his keys from the table and coming to stand in front of me. "Damn, that's too bad." He pulled something from his pocket, but I couldn't take my eyes off of him to see what it was. "I was hoping to give you a chance to earn these back in the car. Another day, I suppose."

Mac kissed the tip of my nose then stepped back, heading toward the door. I caught sight of my lace knickers dangling from his index finger and lunged forward with wide eyes, swiping at them. He held them out of my reach, shite-eating-grin firmly intact.

"Give those back," I demanded.

"Not a chance, sport. I'm going to hang on to these." He tucked them into his pocket then held me back at arm's length by my biceps. Fighting his hold was pointless, so I stopped. "I'll catch you later, tough guy." With that, he stole a quick kiss and left the flat.

◦°◦

"What's the craic?" I asked, slumping into the oversized chair in my sister's living room.

"Are ya fuckin' serious? I haven't seen you in weeks, and you've barely managed to reply to my texts and calls."

Shite. Aoibheann eyed me narrowly from the adjacent

couch. She was fairly cheesed off, and for good reason. It wasn't like me to shut her out as I had. "I'm sorry. I've been an arsehole—"

"That's putting it mildly." She crossed her arms over her chest and cocked a brow at me, daring me to challenge her.

"You're right. I've been a shite brother, and I am sorry. I've had a lot going on."

Her anger melted away to concern, and she uncrossed her arms. "Are you in trouble?"

"No, it's nothin' like that. I…" I squeezed the back of my neck, searching for the right words. No. I was stalling. The right words were right there. "I fell in love."

Her surprised gasp was the only sound in the room. My heart felt like it was going to pound out of my chest, though I sat still with my head high.

"Well, why didn't you tell me sooner, ya eejit?" She waved her hands in front of her in a gesture I hadn't seen from her before. *I guess I shocked her.*

"I didn't realize what was happening until a few nights ago."

She nodded, brushing her bangs behind her ear. "Who is he? What's he like?"

This was the moment I'd been bracing for. I kept my eyes on my sister while I fingered the holes in the knees of my jeans. It was far too hot to be wearing jeans, though I had a feeling I'd have been on fire regardless of what I chose to wear. "It's Mac," I croaked out.

Her brows drew together as she processed my words—as the weight of them sank in. "Mac—as in—"

"Yes."

Aoibheann crossed her arms and leaned back, not once breaking eye contact with me. "Macalister isn't gay, Dubhlainn."

The sigh that left my lips was rueful. "It isn't really my

place to discuss that, though I doubt he'd mind." I swallowed hard, rubbing my now sweaty palms on my thighs. "He's bisexual. We discovered that a few months ago, not long after I moved in." I laid out the events for her, starting with his initial interest, right up to my realization. She remained silent through the entirety of my explanation, which unnerved me. I could count on one hand the number of times my sister was rendered speechless. Those other times had never ended well.

I waited. I'd laid the complete haymes of my life out for her, and I'd wait for her reply—even if it killed me to do so.

After an eternity, Aoibheann sucked in a sharp breath then exhaled it through her mouth on a hum. "Fancy a few scoops?"

I blinked at her like a stunned muppet. "I do. Whiskey would be brilliant."

She got up and motioned for me to follow her, so I did. In the kitchen, I took a seat at the small oak table. My sister set two tumblers and a bottle of Bushmills on the table before joining me. She filled the glasses and pushed one over to me.

"*Sláinte*," we both muttered as we clinked our glasses together, then tossed back the whiskey.

"So," she started, "you're in love with Macalister, *and* he's into fellas now. Grand."

Her tone was flat, neutral even. "You're not angry?"

She shook her head, which did a lot more to calm my nerves than I'd expected. "I understand why you kept it from me, though I really wish you hadn't. I meant what I said about him being a good man. I meant the rest of it too, but it sounds like the two of ye discussed things and didn't entirely jump in blind. I won't lie and say that a part of me doesn't want to get a good dig in on him, but I'll behave."

A snort of laughter had me nearly choking on whiskey. "I'd be worried if you didn't want to."

"What about him? Where does he stand with you?"

I sighed, slumping forward and resting my elbows on the table. "I haven't outright asked him. I don't have to. Mac is… very honest. He was upfront with me about what he wanted from the very start, and I agreed. How I feel now feels like a betrayal to him."

"You can't help who you fall for."

"No, I can't. I could have recognized the signs instead of blissfully ignoring them. I should have—"

"But ya didn't. Stop worryin' about what you could or should have done. All that matters is what you'll do now that you know." She sounded so certain, so confident in her words.

"What should I do?"

She smiled ruefully at me. "I'm sorry, pet. I can't answer that for you."

"Do you think getting involved with him was a mistake?" Part of me didn't want to hear her answer. I knew it was a mistake, I just didn't fuckin' care.

"Not if you're happy. I get that it's not an easy situation, but you have to do what you think is best for you."

I groaned, sliding back against my chair. "I was hoping you'd scold me then tell me what to do. I'm even more conflicted now."

"Sure look it," she replied with a grin.

"There's something else you should know."

She cocked an eyebrow at me, taking another drink. "Oh? Should I give us a refill first?"

"It's nothing bad—at least I hope not. I do drag sometimes. On Friday nights I perform downtown at a bar." After confessing my Mac problem, it only seemed fair to tell Aoibheann everything.

"Shite. You're full of surprises. I hope you know Samir and I will be at your next show. And I *will* kick yer arse if you're prettier than me." Her lips curled into a smile that crinkled the corners of her blue eyes.

I expressed my gratitude while refilling our glasses. Aoibheann had a million questions about drag and preparation, and I was more than happy to answer them all. Knowing I had her full support warmed me more than any whiskey ever could. We spent the rest of the morning on lighter subjects: my upcoming school year, the vacation she and Samir were planning for their one-year wedding anniversary, a particularly frustrating new client she had at work. Our easy exchange helped quiet my inner conflict over what to do about Mac, even if only for a couple of hours.

I didn't have any of the answers I was seeking when I left her house. Even so, I felt better than I had when I'd arrived. Aoibheann had reminded me of all of the things in my life that weren't Mac. I had a renewed sense of perspective that I hoped would help me make the right decision.

o°o

WITH JUST A FEW weeks left before classes resumed, I sat in the middle of my bed with my laptop and tried to make a schedule that wouldn't leave me feeling burnt out. Choosing the classes for my major was easy enough. The electives were the source of my ire. I'd been locked away in my room for almost two hours reading up on courses, and checking where on campus they were located. Building hopping in the snow with minimal time between classes wasn't something I wanted to do again. I made that mistake during my first year.

I was two heartbeats away from flinging my computer onto the floor when I heard a knock at my door. It had to be

Mac. He was out at the table doing his work. I called out for him to come in.

"Dude, are you busy?"

I closed the lid of my laptop, and turned all of my attention on Mac. "Not particularly."

He grinned at me, and I wanted nothing more than to scoot over and invite him into my bed. "Good, because we're going out."

"Where?"

"A magical place where time ceases to exist." My lifted brow and lack of a reply must have burst his positivity bubble. He rolled his eyes while stepping inside my room then motioned around. "It's been like, four months since you moved in, and you still haven't bought any furniture. We're going to IKEA to remedy that. Come on, it's my treat."

I slid out of bed with every intention of marching up to him and telling him that I could damn well buy my own stuff. It was bad enough that Mac paid for most of the bills in the flat. I couldn't have him buying me other shite. The fight bled out of me the second his arms wrapped around my waist and pulled me close. His tender kiss stole my words of protest and brought my dilemma back to the front of my mind.

"You know I love it when you get all feisty, but can you just let me do this? You should at least have a proper dresser or something. I promise it'll be fun."

"Fine. I'll come, but you're not buying it. I can afford to buy a dresser myself."

He squeezed me tighter and hummed. "You know what? I'm taking that as a win. Get dressed." He began to pull away then abruptly stopped. "That feels so wrong to say. I'll remedy that when we get back." With another kiss and a slap to my arse, he was gone.

We survived the nearly hour-long drive in Mac's death trap and ended up having a really fun time at the store. It was my first time at an IKEA, and I hadn't fully grasped how massive the place would be. We spent almost two hours being silly and going through the showroom. Mac had insisted on testing out every single couch and mattress he came across, slowing down our progress. After one look at his puppy-dog eyes, I found myself right next to him every time.

I ended up scrawling down the number of a dresser and a closet organizer for us to pick up on our way out. Mac had insisted we eat first and led me to the restaurant. I tried the Swedish meatballs while Mac got chicken fingers from the kids' menu and three hot dogs. I side-eyed him when he ordered, and again when we sat down. All he did was smile at me and wink in return, insisting that finger food was the best food.

After eating, we went down to the warehouse where Mac handed over a list with three item numbers. I figured he must have found something he liked and didn't spare it another thought. We paid for our items, loaded up the death trap, and headed home.

Lugging those fuckin' boxes up from the car was a right-eous pain in the arse, though I was glad to have Mac with me. On our third trip he'd carried twice as much as me and assured me that his muscles weren't just for show. The bastard.

The boxes for Mac's mystery item were the last to be brought in. They were large, flat, and extremely heavy. With sweat dripping from my forehead, I set the box I'd carried up on the counter and breathed a sigh of relief. "Where do you want these?"

"Your room," he replied.

"What do you mean?"

"I bought you a desk, dude. Classes are starting next

month, and I figured you should have a proper place to study, or write papers, or whatever. You won't always want to use the table out here, and I know I can be loud. Come on, you can smile. Let's skip the part where you pretend to be angry with me and get right to the bashful grin."

I wasn't angry—not at all. I loved that Mac had been thinking about my needs. A desk should have been something I thought of. With a space of my own to work I wouldn't have to spend as much time at the library, allowing me more time with—*do* not *finish that thought.* "Thank you, Mac. I mean it. That was a very thoughtful gift."

"I hope you like it. It's all glass."

I nodded toward the box on the counter. "That explains why these are so fuckin' heavy."

"Yeah, sorry for making you lug your gift up to the apartment." He stepped into my space, and I took a step back, stopping when my back hit the counter. Mac's scruff tickled my jaw while he braced his arms on either side of me on the counter's edge. "I can give you a massage later to work out any kinks you might have. I promise to be impeccably thorough."

"That's the second promise you've made today."

"I kept the first one, didn't I?" He pressed his lips to mine before I could reply, distracting me in the best possible way.

I wanted Mac all over me, though he seemed content with just kissing. I palmed his cock through his shorts while my other hand fisted the back of his hair, holding his mouth to mine. Mac groaned into the kiss then rolled his hips against my hand before stopping himself. He drew back, taking a deep breath through his kiss-swollen lips.

"Fuck, you're intoxicating," he scraped out.

"Then why did you stop?"

"I'm going to fuck your brains out tonight—make no

mistake. I'd really like to do it after we put all that shit together."

"Why not now?"

"We both know I'm going to pass out after I fuck you. I want your stuff to be all ready before that."

Damn him. "You win. If this takes less than an hour, I'll wear anything you want tonight."

His eyes lit up, and he grinned wolfishly. "Anything?" I nodded, stunned when he pushed off the counter and took the box with him. "You're on."

It wasn't a real wager. We both won regardless of the outcome, though I still felt like I was losing. I willed myself to be blissfully ignorant for just a bit longer and followed Mac down the hall.

FIFTEEN

MAC

MY CALVES, THIGHS, AND LUNGS burned from exertion as I ran at a brisk pace on a treadmill. I was sweating buckets, and I didn't even care. I wasn't at the gym in my mind. Instead, I was at home, sprawled out in bed with Dove. The memory from last night was still fresh in my mind—hell, I could almost still feel him against my skin. While watching *Die Another Day* he'd tried to convince me that Daniel Craig was a better Bond than Pierce Brosnan. Kids these days. He had the audacity to say that Craig was even hotter than Brosnan. Now, I considered myself to be a straight man up until a few months ago, but I'd always had a man-crush on Brosnan's Bond. Arguing about it led to wrestling, which inevitably ended up with me pinning Dove with his hands over his head while his hard-on poked my ass.

I shook my head and snickered to myself at the memory. My sudden outburst caught Bryan's attention. He was on my left, also on a treadmill. Maxim ran even less than I did, and was over at the free weights.

"You're thinking about Dubhlainn, aren't you?" Bryan asked with a knowing grin.

"What? How did you know?"

"You're smiling—while doing cardio. You hate cardio. You hate running more than anything, yet here you are with a big dopey smile." The corners of Bryan's mouth lifted, his green eyes glimmering.

"I hate avocado more than running," I muttered.

Bryan snorted a laugh. "Okay, I'll give you that one, but don't try to deny that you were thinking about him."

I pulled the kill switch on my machine and slowed my pace to match until I came to a stop. Bryan did the same, following me over to the benches where we'd set our towels. "I'll own that shit. The kid is a riot. I was just thinking about some stuff he said last night. He tried to come for Brosnan, dude."

Bryan clutched his towel to his chest and gasped with dramatic flair. "He did not."

"Oh, but he did."

"And you're smiling because…?"

I shrugged. "He's adorable. Frustratingly adorable. Sometimes I think he acts contrary just to try and piss me off. Last night definitely turned into one of those times."

Laughter shook Bryan's shoulders as he sat down on the bench and leaned back against the wall. I dropped down next to him and did the same, bumping his knee with mine. "I like seeing you happy, man."

"I'm always happy."

"You know what I mean," Bryan said with a roll of his eyes.

"Do I?"

"The handsome-dunce act really doesn't fit when you're talking to someone who knows you."

"Aw, you think I'm handsome?" Bryan cut his eyes at me, letting me know my humor was not appreciated. "Bry, I genuinely don't know what you're getting at." Well, I had an idea, but I was hoping I was wrong.

A humorless sigh resonated in his throat. "You like Dubhlainn. More than you've been saying. Probably more than you're comfortable admitting, though that doesn't change the fact that it's true. Do you remember last year when you said you were waiting for Eli and me to 'pull our heads out of our asses'? That's what's going on here."

"Whoa, whoa." I held my hands up toward Bryan in the universal sign for wait-just-a-fucking-minute—at least that was what it should have been. "My situation with Dove is *nothing* like what you and Eli went through. Watching you guys was painful, dude. You were both so into each other, and too afraid to act on it."

"And you think this is any different?"

"Of course it is. Dove and I have been upfront with each other. We don't want more than what we've got, and that's fine by me." It had to be, it was my idea, after all. Besides, I was happy. Bryan had been miserable while he pined away for Eli. Unrequited love had made him suffer, and that definitely wasn't me.

"It's not exactly the same as it was with Eli, but it isn't entirely different either. Just like me, you can't see it because you're too close."

I shook my head. "Nope. I'm better at this than you, remember? It was me who gave you advice and pointed you in the right direction. Do you think I wouldn't be able to do the same for myself?"

Bryan nudged me with his shoulder, his gaze turning sympathetic. "You're the best at giving relationship advice, despite having never been in a serious relationship."

"Damn right I am."

"Why do you think that is?"

"Coach don't play," I replied, trying to keep my tone light. I didn't like where Bryan was going with this.

He hummed while nodding, a small grin pulling at his lips. "That's true. But I'm being serious, Mac. I don't mean this the wrong way." He paused for a moment, seemingly at a loss. "I don't think you're able to objectively look at your situation the way you can with others'. If you end up getting hurt because of this—"

"Dove and I are fine, Bry. You don't have to be concerned."

He sighed, slumping his broad shoulders. "Maybe if you keep telling yourself that it'll be true one day. I see now why you didn't tell me what to do back then. You told me I had to realize it for myself, and you were right. I wouldn't have believed you, just as you're doubting me now."

"Come on, don't say it like that. I trust you. I do. I just think you've got it wrong this time." I bumped my knee into his and flashed him a reassuring smile.

"Yeah, okay. If it changes your mind at all, Maxim agrees with me," he said before he got up, heading over to the free weights.

"Wait, you guys talked about me? Did Maxy, like, actually talk? What did he say?"

Bryan flipped me off as he walked away. As amused as I was over the two of them joining forces to help me out, their concern shook me up a bit. What if they were right? Surely I'd know if I wanted more—if Dove wanted more. He wasn't the type to hold back. He'd tell me if things had changed, just as I would for him.

Ugh. This was why I didn't do relationships. This shit was confusing, and I wasn't even in a relationship. Bryan and Maxim were wrong. It was that simple. I joined them over at the free weights, relieved that the topic of discussion had shifted to sports. I pushed my talk with Bryan to the back of my mind and focused on the task at hand and enjoying time with my best friends.

⚬⚬⚬

THE THING about avoiding your thoughts was that they always came back to bite you in the ass. I managed to make it three days without thinking about Bryan's words. Now it was a rainy Wednesday night, and no matter how loud I played my music I couldn't drown out Bryan's voice. Dove was out, and I didn't know where. I'd been distracted with work for most of the day, and had lost track of time. When he wasn't home after the sun had set, I started pondering his where-abouts—and who he could be with. It was stupid, and I knew it. He didn't have to report his whereabouts to me, nor did I expect him to. I trusted that he wasn't out fucking someone else, and the rest wasn't any of my business.

Even so, I couldn't stop myself from wanting to know. I'd thumbed out no fewer than ten messages asking when he might be home and deleted each one. I was *not* going to be that clingy, needy guy. Nope. Not today, Satan.

I tossed my phone onto the couch cushions then continued pacing the living room. I was unusually edgy, and I didn't like it. This wasn't the jealousy I felt in the club, nor was it the same as what I'd felt during Dove's last drag show. Waves of anxiety crashed through me, each one stronger than the last. What started as a niggling "what if" had turned me into a person I didn't recognize in a matter of hours.

What if Bryan and Maxim were right? They weren't, but what if? What if all of this had only been enough because Dove was always here? That was silly. Dove had gone out plenty of times, and it hadn't been a cause for concern. *Yeah, to go to work, see Taylor, or visit his sister.* I'd known where he was every other time. *No.* That couldn't be it. It was ridiculous to think I'd be so worked up just because I didn't know where he was. Missing him shouldn't warrant—

I missed him. More than anything else I was feeling, I missed Dove. My feet stopped—everything did. I shook my head and forced myself to keep walking. I missed him, so what? That didn't mean anything—certainly not what Bryan had said.

A groan rumbled in my throat. I couldn't pace around the apartment all damn night. A bottle of Jameson on the counter caught my eye, and I strode over and snagged it off the counter. I turned the lights out on my way down the hall, stopping at the bathroom. *A bubble bath. What could be more relaxing?* I ran the water nice and hot, and even lit a candle. The flickering tea-light candle provided enough light for me to find the whiskey bottle, which was all I needed.

I'd left my music on in the living room and was being serenaded by Post Malone's "Rockstar." It worked for me.

A quarter of the bottle later, I thought I heard a noise in the living room. The song faded into another, and I didn't catch any other sounds during the brief intermission, so I chalked it up to my imagination. Or the alcohol. I closed my eyes, sinking deeper into the tub and pushing my knees higher above the water's surface.

My candle had gone out about ten minutes ago when I'd accidentally splashed it refreshing the tub with more hot water. I felt around the floor in the dark for the bottle, freezing when the light suddenly lit up the small room. My eyes shot up in time to see Dove jump, clearly startled.

"What the fuck are you doing sitting there in the dark?" he barked out.

I nodded toward the tea-light on the edge of the tub. "My candle got wet."

"You—" He stopped himself then growled. "Never

mind." He turned to leave, and I felt another pang of anxiety rock me.

"Wait!" Dove froze. "Come over here. Please."

Dove sighed then did as asked, standing over me. "What do you want?"

You to stay with me. "You to get naked and get in this tub with me." Dove crossed his arms and looked away, though he hadn't left, so I figured I still had a chance. "I dare you to."

He snorted a laugh. "You think a childish dare is going to get me in the bath with you? You must be off your nut." His gaze dropped to the floor for a moment. "Or half-cut."

"Please, you already know I'm cut—no halves about it," I said with a wide smile.

He quirked a copper brow at me. My dick seemed to like it. "Cock jokes are very unbecoming."

I reached out, hooking my finger through one of the loops on his distressed jeans. "I'll let you choose the music for an entire week if you get in."

That did it. Dove whipped his shirt off, and I unbuttoned his pants, helping him shed them faster. I tried—and failed—not to stare at his naked body. All that smooth, pale skin contrasted with his copper coloring and had me longing to taste him. The semi he was sporting certainly didn't help.

Without me suggesting it, Dove stepped into the tub and slowly lowered himself down with his back to my chest. That inevitably pressed my hardening dick against his ass and lower back, but I couldn't really help that. Dove set his arms on my legs, gripping my raised knees while he let his head fall back on my shoulder.

I took the tie out of his hair, alternating between massaging his scalp and twirling small clumps of his hair around my index finger. As much as I wanted to run my fingers through his hair, I'd learned the hard way that that was a highly romanticized fiction from movies. The reality was that his hair was often tangled if it was up, and it "hurt like a motherfucker" when I snagged my fingers in it. Whoops. Dove had assured me that women with smooth, silky hair had finer hair than his gorgeous wavy locks, or they cheated and brushed it out prior to putting it up.

I didn't mind not being able to run my fingers through it. Touching it like this was more than enough. My efforts were rewarded with Dove's throaty moans, bringing a smile to my face. I kissed his temple, then held out the Jameson, knowing he'd want some. Instead of letting go of me, he winked at me and opened his mouth. I took the hint and poured a generous amount in his mouth before taking a drink of my own. Our breathing fell into sync as we settled into a comfortable silence. My music still filled the apartment, but I couldn't say what song was on.

I didn't ask where he went, nor did he offer the information. Frankly, I didn't care anymore. He was back and in my arms. That was all I needed.

o°o

ON A SUNNY SUNDAY afternoon I walked arm in arm with Grams on a gravel path through the trees. It was too gorgeous of a day to stay inside and shoot the shit, so we drove to a nearby park to… walk around and shoot the shit. I'd invited Dove to come along, though he said he had plans—a common trend this week. The night I had my little freak-out had become a regular thing. Since drowning myself in whiskey every night wasn't exactly healthy, I buried myself in work to stay busy until Dove showed up each night. Once he did, I was then at war with myself over wanting to maw him with affection and respect his privacy and personal space. The latter usually lost out after a few minutes of having Dove within reach. I'd cursed

Bryan countless times for planting those insane ideas in my head.

Leisurely walking around with Grams was doing wonders to keep my mind from straying to unwanted places. I told her all about the wager I made with Dove, and that I bought him a desk for his studies. I left out how much of a head case I was whenever he went out—Grams didn't need to worry about me over nothing.

"You should have seen how happy he was when I finished setting the desk up. He was practically vibrating with joy. It was the cutest thing ever." I smiled to myself as I told the story—something I did often according to Bry. "I even told him as much, which I'm sure you can guess didn't end so well for me. He's small, but the dude packs a punch when he means it," I said, rubbing my bicep where he'd hit me to gain sympathy.

Instead of consoling her dear grandson, Grams playfully slapped my arm where I'd indicated Dove had punched me. "You're lucky he didn't go for your face. You tease that boy too much."

"Nah, I like to think I tease him just enough."

"You haven't stopped talking about him today." Her tone shifted, taking on a casual inflection. I knew this trick from years of exposure: she wanted to talk about something serious without making it sound like a lecture. I didn't understand why she was using it now.

"Is that so?"

"It is, dear."

I thought back on what I had shared, and yeah, everything had involved Dove. "He's my roommate. It's unavoidable, I suppose."

"You didn't talk about Bryan nearly as much, and you certainly didn't smile nonstop while doing so." She tilted her head toward me, cocking an eyebrow.

I shrugged. "Is everyone around me a psychoanalyst now? You're reading too much into things."

Grams dropped my arm and stopped walking. "Watch your sass and quit deflecting."

I set my hands on my hips and groaned. Why was this happening to me? "I'm not deflecting—"

"You are."

A couple walking by with a stroller caught my attention behind Grams. The woman quickly turned away when our eyes met. *Great. Now the whole park knows about my drama.* I turned back to Grams and let out a heavy sigh. "Can we have this discussion somewhere with at least a shred of privacy?"

Grams agreed, and I led her over to a shaded bench just off the main path. Neither of us said anything at first. This was her idea, and I had every intention of waiting her out. So I waited.

And waited.

And wai— "Okay, I can't take it anymore."

"I've been playing the waiting game since before your father was born. You honestly didn't expect you'd win, did you?"

I knew damn well that was a rhetorical question. I leaned back, lacing my fingers behind my head, and stared at the sky through the leaves and branches. "Tell me whatever's on your mind."

"No, dear. *You* tell me."

"I don't know what you want me to say, Grams. I won't sit here and say I don't like Dove, because I clearly do. I enjoy his company quite a bit."

She turned toward me, resting an elbow on the back of the bench. "How do you feel when you're with him?"

"Happy. He's a lot of fun to be around," I answered easily.

Grams nodded. "What about when he's not around?"

I swallowed hard, though my mouth was suddenly dry as fuck. She couldn't have noticed that I was absolutely *hating* being away from him. "It sucks. I get bored. I, ah, I miss him sometimes."

"Is that all?"

I brought my hands down, linking my fingers in my lap to keep from squirming. This was Grams—I could tell her anything. "I miss him a lot. It's… all I can think about at times. Ever since Bryan planted that stupid idea in my head that there was something more going on I haven't been able to relax when he's not around. It almost makes me feel sick to my stomach, which I know is ridiculous."

Grams squeezed my clasped hands, flashing me a sympathetic smile. "It's not ridiculous."

"I don't like it. I can't relax if I don't know when he's coming back. When he does"—I frowned, searching for the right words—"I feel this consuming rush of relief spread through me, and all the stress and anxiety is gone. It's like…"

"Like you're yourself again."

"Fuck. That's exactly it. How did you know?"

"That's how I felt whenever I was reunited with your grandfather, love."

I shook my head and laughed dryly. "I don't like it. I don't recognize myself when I get like that. I feel uncertain of everything except how much I want him near me. Everything else feels grossly unimportant and lackluster."

An amused hummed reached my ears. Grams's eyes were full of unshed tears. "That's love, Macalister."

My stomach churned as a wave of nausea settled over me. I gripped the edge of the bench and leaned forward, breathing in through my nose and exhaling through my mouth. Grams rubbed one hand in small circles on my back while the other stroked my hair behind my ear.

"Are you okay?"

"Yes. No." I shook my head, unsure of what else to do. "I don't know."

She continued to soothe me while she encouraged me to tell her what I was thinking. I couldn't possibly convey all of my thoughts coherently. I'd accepted being bisexual like it was nothing, yet this realization had me reeling. It wasn't that Dove was a guy; I just never expected to feel… however the hell I felt about him. It was unlike anything I'd ever felt before, though I wasn't ready to rush and call it love—not until I was certain.

"I don't know if it's love. I mean, I haven't been in love before, so I just don't know. I'm not ready to debate the semantics of what love is. What I am sure of is that I want Dove. I want him more than I've ever wanted anything. Ugh, I sound like a sap." My eyes stung, and I sniffled to rein my emotions in. I was not going to fucking cry in the middle of the park. "I hate that everyone else was right. Bryan isn't going to let me live this down."

Grams hummed, smiling broadly at me. "Don't worry about that right now. What are you going to do about your newfound realization?"

That was easy. I met Grams's firm yet comforting gaze and matched her smile with one of my own. "I need to tell him. I should probably wait until I've figured my shit out so I don't sound like an idiot, but I think he should know. I want him to know." I wanted to tell him in that instant, though I wasn't about to take off and leave Grams on the bench. She insisted I could cut my visit short, but I refused to leave. I could talk to Dove when I got home. Hopefully by then I'd have a better idea of what I'd say.

The sun had already set by the time I got home. I tossed my keys on the table by the door then immediately sought out Dove. He was lying on the couch watching TV, though he'd muted it after I came in. Before my nerve abandoned me, I strode over to the couch, arriving as he sat up. My lips parted, and I was about to tell him everything—then he beat me to it.

"Mac, we need to talk."

My mouth snapped shut. Five simple words could mean anything, though Dove's solemn tone and the set of his jaw told me I wasn't going to like what he had to say. The urge to confess everything to him still brimmed within me, ready to overflow at any moment. As much as I wanted to speak, I needed to hear him out first.

"What about?" I managed to ask, sounding casual enough.

Dove stood, though he kept an uncomfortable distance between us. He buried his hands in his pockets, looking down at his bare feet before back up at me. I wanted to go to him—to pull him close and make him smile, but everything about his demeanor screamed for me to keep my distance. "I want to end things," he finally said.

Five more words. Five more fucking words, and I felt like I'd been rocked by Mike Tyson. It took all of my resolve not to stagger back. It was possible that I'd heard him wrong, or maybe he wasn't talking about us. Foolishly hopeful, I chewed on my inner cheek before asking him, "What do you mean by that?"

"Our arrangement. I want to end it. Now." His voice came out steady. It sounded so… final.

To say I was shocked would be an egregious understatement. I was a lot of things in that moment, though hurt and confused seemed to be at the top of the list.

SIXTEEN

DUBHLAINN

T HIS WASN'T GOING HOW I'd envisioned. I'd expected Mac to try to sway me with the lure of sex, or to make a joke about how his dick had ruined me for all others. He did neither of those things. When I'd told him I wanted to end things for the second time I could have sworn that he looked stricken. It was gone in a flash, and I wasn't convinced that I hadn't imagined it. Maybe it was some sick part of my mind projecting onto him. *I'm a fuckin' mess; why shouldn't you be too?*

No. That wasn't what I wanted. I was ending things before they turned to shite. It fuckin' sucked, but at least this way both of us wouldn't be miserable when this exploded in our faces. I wanted to spare him that. It would be hard, though I knew I could take it. I always did. What I couldn't take was Mac hating me or feeling like I'd betrayed his trust. That would kill me.

"Why?" he finally asked with his hands on his hips and his brow furrowed.

"It isn't working for me anymore. It's not what I truly want." It wasn't a lie. I hoped I was vague enough to not alert him of my true feelings, but sincere enough that he wouldn't see through me. I expected some pushback because, well, that was just how Mac was. What I wasn't prepared for was another look of vulnerability from him. He schooled his expression just as fast as the first time, though there was no mistaking it the second time. It fuckin' gutted me. Why had he looked so sad? I wanted to comfort him—to take back my twisted words and tell him the full truth. Instead I stood several feet from him with my hands balled into fists in my pockets, and I pretended to be strong. I pretended what I was doing wasn't hurting me.

Mac nodded, rubbing the back of his neck. "Okay. If that's what you want."

"Aye. It is."

"Okay," he repeated, dazed almost. "All right. I guess it had to end sometime, right? Better now than later when I've ruined you for good—am I right?" He smiled at me, though it didn't reach his beautiful brown eyes. He cracked another joke then excused himself, stating he needed a shower to get rid of the swamp ass he'd been suffering through all afternoon. I watched him leave the room with a weak half smile, exhaling for what felt like the first time when he closed the bathroom door behind him.

He'd sounded like himself, but something was off. I'd seen him actin' the maggot plenty of times, and this was different. I turned my show off and quietly went to my room, glancing at the bathroom door as I passed it. Mac hadn't had the same carefree conviction in his words, though he was trying. For me? No. I probably wounded his pride.

I climbed into my bed, clutching a pillow to my chest—the one that smelled like Mac. I closed my eyes and breathed in his scent, letting myself have this one concession until I did laundry in the morning. If wounding his pride was the worst of the damage I'd done, then I'd gladly take that over my other fears.

◦º◦

I WELCOMED the distraction my classes brought me. I'd been back to school for two thrilling weeks. Between that and working at the supermarket I was kept ridiculously busy. I even had to forgo performing at the club, though my heart wouldn't have been in it, anyway. The vast majority of any time I spent at the flat was in my room. The desk Mac got for me became my new best friend; I spent more time sitting at it than I did in my bed. When I wasn't working or studying I would still sit at the desk, staring aimlessly out the window.

I barely saw Mac anymore. I heard him moving about the flat, but I never had the balls to go out and face him. He was pleasant and didn't seem angry when he saw me, which only made me feel like more of an arsehole. I'd ended things with him so they wouldn't go to shite later, though all I accomplished was tearing a rift between us. It was exactly like it had been when I first moved in, except Mac wasn't pursuing me, and somehow that was a kick in the bollocks. I'd lost him as a lover, and I felt him slip further away daily as my mate. The more I pushed him away, the less he tried.

I couldn't fault him for that. As far as he knew, we'd been having a brilliant time together then I went and pissed all over it. I didn't know what I'd expected to happen, but this wasn't it. Our relationship was shite now, and I hadn't the slightest clue how to fix it.

So I sat at my desk—sometimes for hours. I watched all the people and cars go by while I felt stuck. Mac didn't hate me—I'd succeeded in preventing that from coming to pass.

We were in a different shite place, and I found myself questioning how much better that truly was.

⊙⁰⊙

ON THE THIRD Friday in September I'd managed to catch up on all of my assignments, and had the night free. I called Taylor to inquire about performing, relieved when he told me I was going on at ten. I'd had enough of being me. Renée Steady was everything I needed to be and fell short of. Where she was strong and confident, I was weak and unsure of myself. I knew drag wasn't the answer to my problems with Mac, but one night off from my misery sounded brilliant.

I called Aoibheann next, letting her know about the show. She'd replied that it was bloody late, but that she and Samir would be there to cheer me on. A smile tugged at the corners of my mouth from knowing I had their support. I still had Taylor too, though I hadn't seen him since classes started back up—something else to add in support of me being the world's biggest arsehole.

We made lunch plans for tomorrow then disconnected. Leaning back in my desk chair, I did a scan of my room, settling on the wall I shared with Mac's room. He'd been spending more time out, which wasn't like him at all. Mac loved to lounge around at home more than almost anything, yet he was hardly ever around anymore.

When I got in late some nights I'd stop by his door and listen for his breathing. More often than not, it wasn't there. Then it struck me that he was probably out getting some arse like he did before we got involved. I should have been relieved that he did it outside of the flat, but I wasn't. It was selfish of me, though that didn't stop me from feeling slighted.

I got up and walked over to the shared wall, pressing my ear against the cool surface. Nothing. It was Friday night—of course he wouldn't be home. Instead of letting myself dwell on what he could be doing and whom he was doing it with, I marched back over to my desk and grabbed my phone. I typed out a quick message for Taylor, asking if I could come over early, then I packed up my things I'd need for the show and left the flat.

"It's been a while, gorgeous," Taylor said as he welcomed me into his flat.

"I know. I'm sorry. Everything has been so hectic this month."

"You don't have to explain." Taylor close the door behind me then eyed me closely, wrinkling his nose. "Cancel that—you *do* have to explain. You look like shit."

"Thanks for being so tactful."

"Tact has no place here, sis." One corner of his lush lips lifted in a grin before his expression turned somber. "This wouldn't have something to do with a certain hunky blond, would it?"

"I wish I could say it didn't," I replied ruefully.

Taylor nodded, his hands suddenly holding one of mine. "Come, come. I bet there's a story here."

We skipped the couch, heading straight for his bed instead. Taylor pulled back the covers and motioned for me to get in first, which I did. He crawled in, facing me, and gave me an encouraging smile. I laid everything out for him —from my feelings for Mac to how awful I felt being alone in our flat. Taylor listened to every word without judgment. Even when I cringed over how awful something I felt sounded out loud, Taylor just nodded and let me talk.

By the time I was finished I felt marginally better and was able to tell Taylor as much when he asked. "Of course you feel better," he started. "Keeping shit bottled up is the worst thing you can do. It doesn't matter what your feelings are—you have to get them out, sis."

I nodded, unable to deny his words. "Thanks, Dr. Taye."

"Anytime, Irish. I accept payment in the form of Louboutin stilettos—I wear a forty-two," he said with a wink.

"Bloody hilarious," I deadpanned, eliciting a self-satisfied laugh from Taylor.

"Do you know what you're going to do tonight? It's kind of last minute."

"'Ex-Girlfriend' by No Doubt."

"No shit, huh?" Taylor asked with a sympathetic grin.

I attempted a smile, though it didn't reach my eyes. "Lucky for me there's a No Doubt or Gwen song for every occasion."

"Enough." Taylor clapped his hands twice. "We have hours before we have to be anywhere—I say we order some pizza and binge on *Untucked*. I've even got ice cream."

A genuine smile pulled at my lips, and I nodded. "That sounds brilliant."

The next morning I was in the kitchen making bacon, baked beans, fried tomatoes, and eggs. It wasn't quite a full Irish breakfast, though it was the best I could do with what we had. I'd heard Mac come in late last night and wanted to try to patch things up with him. He loved food, so breakfast seemed like a good peace offering.

I was finishing up the bacon when Mac entered the kitchen, rubbing the sleep from his eyes.

"Good morning," I said with what I hoped was an easy smile.

Mac ran a hand down his bare stomach and scratched just beneath the band of his blue kex. I tried not to stare at his body, but I failed miserably. It had been weeks since I'd seen this much of him, and my eyes were drinking him in, stocking up for the next drought.

He flashed me a sleepy grin and wished me a good morning in return. I turned back to the sizzling bacon, relieved that our small exchange hadn't been awkward. Mac's footsteps came nearer until he stood beside me. As I turned to ask him what he was doing, his fingers gently twisted in the loose dangling stands of my hair. He brought it to his nose and softly inhaled, humming contentedly.

I froze, completely unsure of what else to do. My grip on the spatula tightened when Mac's beard tickled my ear. "Mac," I whispered gently.

His fingers stilled while my heart hammered in my chest. He dropped the locks of my hair and stepped back. His eyes were wide, and he appeared a bit disoriented. "I… I'm sorry, Dubhlainn. I don't know—that won't happen again."

I flinched at his use of my full name, disguising it with a nod. He was the only person who called me Dove, and I missed it. "It's all right. Breakfast will be ready shortly."

He bowed his head once then backed away, taking a seat at the table. He opened his laptop and didn't spare me another glance all through breakfast.

So much for patching things up.

LUNCH with my sister gave me a much-needed excuse to get out of the flat. Mac hadn't retreated to his room, though the silent treatment was just as rough. I met up with Aoibheann at a small pub a few blocks from her office. The place was an absolute dive, though the pints were cheap. I didn't even have to use my fake ID.

I'd kept Aoibheann up to date on my situation with Mac

via text. She didn't bring him up at all during our meal, which was refreshing. She mostly told me how much fun she and Samir had at the show, surprised at the energy in the room.

"You were nearly unrecognizable—and prettier than me, you little shite."

I smirked, finishing my third pint. "I've always been the pretty one."

"Fancy yourself a gas lad today, I see."

"I'm just callin' it like I see it."

Halfway through my next pint, Aoibheann suddenly smiled wide and waved to someone behind me. I turned in my chair, locking eyes with Eli. I nodded to him then faced my sister. "I should get going."

She placed her hand over mine on the table, squeezing gently. "Stay. It's just Eli. Bryan or Mac aren't coming."

"No. I've got a few things I need to do today."

"Like what?" she asked in a challenge.

Eli arrived at the table and greeted us, flashing me a shy smile. He had to know what was going on with me and Mac. From what I understood, there was very little Mac withheld from Bryan, and nothing that Bryan wouldn't share with his fiancé. I knew that my presence would have Eli's anxiety on high and put him in an awkward spot—all of which would be easily avoided if I left.

"I'm sorry for interrupting," he said to me, then turned to Aoibheann. "I'm a little early. I was just over at the bakery and left too soon."

"It's okay, pet. Have a seat," she replied with a smile.

"Don't worry about it. I was just leaving." My sister's cocked eyebrow leveled me. "I'm getting a haircut if you *must* know. I need a change, and it's too hot for this length." That was a lie. The last official day of summer was last week, and the high temperatures were already falling off. She didn't call me out, though. She and Eli didn't need to know that I was cutting my hair so Mac wouldn't be tempted to touch it again. He loved my hair, and maybe he'd lose some of his lingering interest if it was gone.

I finished my pint before excusing myself then wandered around until I found a barber. I loved my hair, and had been growing it out for years. It had become part of my identity, and I was scared as hell to cut it. I sat down in the barber's chair and reminded myself that my hair would always grow back, which was more than I could say for some things.

SEVENTEEN

MAC

Т HE THING ABOUT SADNESS was that it came in waves. The last time I'd been remotely upset was when my grandpa passed, and what I felt now was too similar to that. It was exacerbated by the fact that I still had to see Dove daily and pretend that I was okay. So I did what I had to. I put on a smile and pretended that my beating heart hadn't been ripped out of my chest by the person who lit up my world.

It was a solid plan, though I failed on the execution. The morning after I'd been essentially dumped, I saw Dove in the kitchen and couldn't muster more than a weak "hi." He seemed equally uncomfortable and returned to his room for the rest of the day. After that I stopped trying. It was clear that there was going to be an adjustment period for us both —though for extremely different reasons.

I spent more time at the office and visiting home and Grams. After four days of consecutive visits home I told Miho what had happened and almost burst into tears. I managed to hold it in, keeping on a brave face for my baby sister. That didn't stop her from crying for me. My mom had been eavesdropping on that conversation and burst into my room. Also crying. I'd filled Dad in while he was cooking.

The hardest person to talk to—aside from Dove—was Grams. She felt awful for the way things turned out, though she insisted I try to talk to him again. I couldn't see the point. He'd outright told me sleeping with me wasn't what he wanted, and I had to respect that. Losing the sexual aspect of a relationship sucked, but it was low on the list of painful, stabby things. What I missed most was his companionship. Just being around him, talking, laughing, holding him— those things I'd taken for granted when my head was firmly buried in the sand. I missed my friend. I missed the warmth of a lover I never truly had.

Two weeks in and I wasn't getting over being a mopey asshole, so I decided to put more distance between us. I'd showed up on Maxim's doorstep with a duffel and crashed a few nights on his couch. He didn't ask me any questions, though that didn't stop me from eventually spilling the story. On my first morning back at home in almost a week I'd fucked up royally. Dove was making breakfast and he'd seemed happy to see me. I'd honestly thought I was still asleep, and I'd touched him in a way I had no right to do anymore. I'd played with his hair and was about to kiss his neck and tell him how much I missed him. He'd stopped me then, shattering my fantasy and bringing me back to my colorless reality. The worst part was that he'd come home with a haircut. It wasn't just a trim—his loose copper waves now stood up, no longer weighed down by their length. The cut was shorter on the sides, drawing the eye to the mess of loose curls on top. He looked fucking gorgeous, but knowing that my slipup had been the reason he'd cut it was another stab.

Forget about fucking him—he didn't want me to touch him whatsoever. I left again after that, going back to my parents' house until my mom's never-ending babying drove me crazy. She only ever fussed over me when I was sick, and I guess being heartbroken counted.

The most recent stop on my pity-train was Bryan and Eli's apartment, which I'd been putting off since they were happy and planning their wedding, and I just didn't want to ruin that. Bryan guessed as much and called me, all but demanding I get my sorry ass over to see them.

That was three days ago. It was the last Friday in September, and I was spending it in my boxers, sprawled out on their couch with Prince lying on my chest. Bryan was cooking something with a lot of garlic and lemon. Eli alternated between sitting on a stool at the kitchen island to talk to Bryan and at the foot of the couch. I knew he was babysitting me, but I didn't care.

He and Bryan were in the kitchen speaking in hushed tones while I watched videos on my phone of a certain drag queen. Some were my own private videos, but I found so many more on the YouTube channel for the club and spectator uploads. I didn't let myself watch them often, but I was feeling pathetic and missing him.

I jumped, startling Prince, when I saw that the club had uploaded a new video from last Friday. I watched Dove strut around to a familiar No Doubt song, looking every bit as vibrant and sexy as he did for all of his shows. A small grin lifted the corners of my mouth as I watched. He wore another bright pink wig and had the most dramatic makeup I'd seen him in to date. My smile faded when the chorus reminded me of which song this was: "Ex-Girlfriend." I closed the app, locked my phone, and tossed it on the table in front of the couch, causing a louder bang than I'd intended.

Eli was in front of me within seconds. He sat down on

the floor with his legs crossed, putting him almost at eye level with me. "Is everything okay?" he asked gently.

"No, it's not," I snapped.

He winced, and I felt like an asshole. "I'm sorry. I should have worded that better."

I sighed, raking my teeth over my top lip. "Shit, I'm sorry, Eli. I didn't mean to take my shit out on you. I… don't feel like myself. One of the videos I was watching just set me off." I reached out and lifted his chin with the knuckle of my index finger. "Seriously, don't feel bad. Well, you can feel bad for me if you want to, but don't think you did anything wrong."

He grinned then nodded his head. "I saw Dubhlainn last week." He paused, studying my face for my reaction. "I wasn't going to mention it because I didn't want to upset you. He was with Eve. I think you should try talking to him again."

I furrowed my brow at that. "He doesn't want to talk to me."

"Are you sure? He seemed… I don't know… sad. He bolted pretty fast after I showed up—he said something about wanting a haircut. It wasn't like him. He's never been weird with me before, but that felt weird."

I barked out a humorless laugh, recalling that day in the kitchen when I thought I'd been having the sweetest dream. "Do you know why he got a haircut?"

"He said it was too hot for that much hair."

My jaw clenched. I rubbed Prince behind her ears in an attempt to relax. "That morning I'd accidentally touched his hair. I used to do it all the time. I honestly thought I was dreaming. He flinched when I said his name. Like, physically recoiled. I felt like such a scumbag."

"Mac, I'm sorry. I shouldn't have said anything."

His eyes were welling up with tears, and I wanted to reassure him, but my mouth was too dry to speak. In a few quick strides, Bryan was next to his fiancé, holding a hand out for him and pulling him up. He pulled Eli into a hug, kissed his temple, and whispered in his ear. I didn't want to intrude on their intimate moment, but I was kind of stuck on the couch with Prince on top of me. Eli nodded and was smiling when Bryan pulled back.

"Come on, girl," Eli called for Prince. She jumped off of me and followed him to the front door. I heard some shuffling, the clicking of her leash being hooked onto her collar, and finally the door opening and closing.

With Eli gone, Bryan crossed his arms and turned his attention on me. "Mac—"

"I didn't mean to upset him."

Bryan shook his head. "He's all right. Sit up and scoot over." I did as instructed, and Bryan sat down next to me with his body angled toward mine. He eyed me for a moment before shaking his head again. "You look like shit."

I scratched at my beard—it was in definite need of trimming. A haircut probably wouldn't hurt either. "I feel like shit. I feel like a pathetic mess."

"You only just realized what you wanted before it was ripped away; you're allowed to hurt, man."

"Hurting is one thing. I sit around watching videos of him and listen to 'Nothing Compares 2 You' like a heartbroken fool."

Bryan snorted. "You *are* a heartbroken fool." He nudged me with his elbow, grinning. "Prince or Sinéad O'Connor?"

"You know I love Prince, but it's been O'Connor. You know—the whole Irish thing."

He hummed, leaning against me and hitching his feet up onto the couch. The citrus smell from the kitchen was strong on him. "It's a great song either way."

"I tried watching some porn."

"This is news now?" Bryan asked with a playful grin.

"Gay porn, you douche." We were both well aware that I'd seen gay porn before. With having a gay best friend, and the two of us—namely me—having no boundaries, it was bound to happen on occasion over the years. And it did, though we both knew this was different.

"And?"

"It made me feel depressed. Horny and depressed," I admitted.

"So it's not just Dùbhlainn." It wasn't a question.

I shook my head. "No, it's not. I guess I have a type too when it comes to guys. The ones that looked like me or bigger weren't really doing it for me. None of the guys came close to having the effect on me he does, though."

"That's because you love him, you dork. It has nothing to do with the way he looks."

I draped my arm over Bryan's chest, feeling oddly comforted by the rise and fall. "I miss doing this with you, Bry. Don't get me wrong, I'm elated that you and Eli are moving forward, and I'd have kicked your ass if you stayed living with me instead of moving in with him. I still miss just hanging out like this."

He craned his neck to look up at me, his pale green eyes meeting mine. "I do too." He quietly chuckled to himself, then looked away.

"What's so funny?"

"I was just thinking about what Miho would say if she could see us right now."

"Oh, God. She doesn't need this much ammo. Right after I came out she actually asked me if we ever made out—right at the damn dinner table."

Bryan's chest shook under my hand as laughter erupted from him. "Shit. You didn't tell her about Vegas, did you?"

"Are you fucking crazy? She'd never let that go. She'd get

herself ordained online and probably marry us behind our backs." We both shared a laugh at that, knowing it was the very least my little sister would do. "Did you tell Eli?"

"Yeah, I did. He actually cried laughing. Don't worry, though. I made him promise not to tell anyone."

"I'm not worried about that. I know he can keep a secret."

A comfortable silence fell between us with the only sound in the apartment coming from a simmering pot on the stove. I glanced around the space that had once exclusively been Eli's. It now had elements of Bryan and the life they shared. A framed photo of the two of them hanging on the wall by the window caught my eye more than anything else. It was one I'd taken last year at Thanksgiving after they'd officially started dating.

"Hey, Bry," I started quietly. "How did you know Eli was 'the one'?"

He thought it over for several beats, his breaths coming in sharper when I thought he might speak but didn't. "Simply put, I couldn't imagine being happy without him. He helped me experience everything in a new light, and I wanted that forever. It took a while, but once he opened up to me as friends I knew I was fucked. Everything he did, he did so earnestly—even if he was a bit blunt or awkward at times."

I snorted. "I can't imagine him *not* being blunt and awkward."

"Right? I admired the honest person he was, and I wanted to be someone important to him. Someone he could trust and depend on. Maybe even someone he could love," he said shyly.

"Damn, dude."

"Yep."

"I don't want to continue feeling like this. Tiptoeing around Dove is killing me."

"What are you going to do about it?" Bryan asked.

"Your man was right; I should talk to him again. Even if the outcome is the same, or worse. I don't want to be the guy who runs from his problems. I was ready to tell him that I wanted to be with him. I can accept that he doesn't want me in return, but I need to tell him—for me." It was almost foreign to my ears, but for the first time in weeks I sounded confident. This was something I absolutely knew I had to do.

Bryan held up his fist, which I bumped with mine. "There's my Mac. I missed you, dude. When are you going to tell him?"

"Right now—well, whenever he gets home."

Bryan sat up, and I went to stand, only to be pushed back down. "Hold up. I dig your gusto here, but please go shower and shave first. Eli is too polite to tell you you're a mess, but I meant it when I said you looked like shit." The corner of his mouth lifted into a half grin, and his eyes shone.

"Fine. I'm using your electric razor, though." I jumped up with renewed spirits. I wasn't under the delusion that my confession would change Dove's mind, but I hoped it would allow us to be able to move past the horrible place we were in.

"By all means," Bryan said as the door opened.

Eli and Prince had returned from what I guessed was a short run, given the color on Eli's cheeks. I changed my course from the bathroom to the front door and planted a giant kiss on Eli's cheek. "Thank you," I said to him before running for the bathroom, dodging Bryan as he tried to grab me. I locked the door behind me, taunting Bry as he demanded I unlock it. Yeah, it was good feeling like me again.

᷈

I'D WAITED for about two hours before Dove came home. His eyes widened when he saw me sitting on one of the island stools with my arms crossed, angled toward the door. "Hi," he managed, voice tight and uncomfortable.

I wasn't deterred. I knew this was what I had to do, and nothing could shake me. I'd already had my heart broken; all I could do from here was heal—and hopefully fix my friendship with Dove in the process. "Hey, kiddo. Do you have a minute? There's something I've needed to say to you for the past few weeks."

Unlike the first time I called him that, he seemed almost happy at the nickname. He nodded and took a seat at the stool next to mine that I motioned to. "I want you to know that what I'm about to say isn't an attempt to sway you one way or the other, and I apologize if it upsets you."

His forehead creased, though he nodded again and remained silent. "That day you told me you wanted to end our arrangement was one of the worst days of my life. I was too fucking blind and ignorant to realize what everyone around me already knew. Grams got through to me, and it hit me hard that what I felt for you went beyond normal feelings for a friend or fuck buddy." His back stiffened, and I licked my lips, determined to lay it all out for him. "I came home with the intention of telling you that I might be in love with you. It was brand new, so I wasn't one hundred percent sure. Now I am. I haven't been in love before, but I know this has to be it—you're it for me, Dove."

I flicked my gaze down at my shaking hands for a moment, clenching them into fists. When I looked back up at Dove his cheeks were flushing, and he stared back at me, his eyes burning me up. "I'm so fucking gone for you," I admitted, my voice cracking. I cleared my throat and brushed my nose, willing myself not to cry. I wasn't trying to guilt him with an overly emotional display. "I respect that the same isn't the case for you. I hope we can get back—"

The screeching of the stool across the floor cut me off. Dove was up and walking past me in a flash. He looked mad as hell. I got up and took two steps toward him before I stopped myself. He spun around and pinned me from across the room with those pale, crystal-blue eyes. His chest heaved, and his lips parted. The air in the room felt charged. I half expected him to come at me with his fist clenched—then he did. He charged me; only instead of punching me he jumped up, and wrapped himself around me. My hands were on him just as quickly as his lips crashed against mine. He worked his hands through my overgrown hair as his tongue worked its way into my mouth, claiming me. Too caught up in the moment—in him, I forgot to breathe. I pulled back on a gasp, enjoying how his lips had gone from their usual pink to a deeper shade. He rubbed his cheek along my freshly trimmed jaw, and I thanked Bryan for going all "dad" on me and forcing me to shave.

"Is this really happening?" he asked, his eyes closed and forehead resting against mine.

"I think that's my line."

He laughed, though it came out more like a shudder. "I mean it. Tell me this is real."

I tilted his chin up, and he opened his glassy eyes. "I love you. This is very real for me."

His lips trembled as a few tears stained his cheeks. "Say it again."

"I love you, Dove."

"I love you too, you fuckin' dope," he said before he kissed me again.

I matched his ferocity, and spun us around to set him on

the counter. I brushed the backs of my fingers over his dampened cheeks and smiled. "I've missed you so much."

"I'm so sorry, Mac. I thought I was doing the right thing. I was wrong, and I'm so fuckin' sorry." Fresh tears fell from his eyes, and I pulled him against me again. "Don't let go—not yet," he whispered in my ear, his arms wrapped tight around my neck.

"You kidding? I'm never letting you go now." I picked him up and carried him down to my bedroom, gently laying him on my bed. I lowered myself over him, thrilled when I felt his hands on me, pulling me closer to him.

"I want you," he rasped before he bit my earlobe. "I want you so fuckin' bad." He worked a hand into my jeans, cupping my balls and stiffening cock.

I shuddered and rutted against his hand. I pushed myself up so I was straddling his hips, and took off his shirt and then my own. I ran my hands over every inch of exposed skin I could find, mapping his body and committing it to memory. My fingers stilled when I reached the button on his jeans.

"I haven't been with anyone else," I said, my voice thick with a consuming need for him.

He kissed my fingertips then smiled. "Neither have I."

I nodded, a tear or two finally falling from my eyes. I hadn't realized just how much I'd needed to hear those words, though Dove seemed to know how important they were. He sat up then brushed my tears away with his thumb before he kissed my closed eyes. My hands skimmed up his bare sides until I had his copper curls between my fingers. I closed the short distance between us, kissing him gently and without any urgency. We lay back down and shed the remainder of our clothes, enjoying the feel of skin-to-skin contact.

When I finally entered him, it was slow and somehow so

much more than just sex. For the first time in my life, I made love to someone. Our fingers were entwined and our lips never separated as we moved together in a slow rhythm. Dove bit my bottom lip, moaning against my mouth as he came. Two more deep, measured thrusts, and I was spilling into him as my orgasm rocked through me from my toes to my fingers locked with Dove's.

We panted, our short breaths mingling, and I couldn't help but smile. I had Dove *back*. In a way, I had him for the first time. I knew what it felt like to lose him, and I was determined to never let that come to pass again. I kissed him again then slowly pulled out and lay down next to him. He rolled toward me, resting his head on my arm, and was asleep within minutes.

We had a lot to talk through, but it could wait until morning came. I was exhausted, and clearly Dove was right there with me. Pulling him closer, I kissed the top of his head and let myself drift into the first peaceful sleep I'd had in what felt like years.

o°o

A FEW DAYS LATER, I called for a family dinner and requested that Grams make the trip over for it. Dove and I had had plenty of time to talk through our feelings, and things couldn't have been better. I wanted to introduce him to my family as my boyfriend. My partner. It still sounded crazy to me, but in a good, exciting way.

Dove had called Eve the morning after we made things official. I heard her happy scream from across the room, and had received a threatening text from her moments after they ended their call. She'd promised me bodily harm, potentially resulting in the loss of life if I broke his heart—the same thing I'd send to any guy dumb enough to try to date my baby sister. I sent her a snarky reply to rile her up, though I had every intention of sitting her down and reassuring her that I was serious about her brother.

I sat on my childhood bed, leaning back on my arms as I watched Dove. He stood in front of my closed door, eyeing my huge Jean Grey poster. "What's up?" I asked him.

He shrugged. "It's stupid."

I sat up, reaching an arm out for him. He came to me and sat in my lap—something he'd started doing a lot. I liked it. A lot. "What're you thinking?"

"I shouldn't have cut my hair. I knew how much you loved it. I was being a stubborn arse."

"You did what you thought you had to. It's all right now. Besides, I like the short do. It's cute as hell, and now"—I ran my fingers through his soft, loose curls—"I get to do this whenever I want. If you want it long again, you can grow it back out."

"Do you have any idea how long I'd been growing it out?" he whined.

"Hopefully a long-ass time. I want to be around when it's that length again," I replied with a wink. He smiled, though it faded faster than I liked. "What else is bothering you?"

"You love Jean Grey," he said dejectedly. He motioned to his hair, sighing. "I don't look like her anymore."

Uuf. Be still, my heart. "I didn't fall for you because you looked like a fictional character." He narrowed his eyes at me, quirking an eyebrow. "Fuck, okay. So I was super attracted to your hair in the beginning. Cut me some slack—I love your feisty ass now. Besides, you still look like Jean Grey. *Uncanny X-Force* volume 1, issue nineteen-point-one: *The Age of Apocalypse.* Jean Grey has the exact same haircut as you do right now, and I'm being honest when I say that I like it better on you." I snuck a quick kiss while he flushed and laughed.

"Jaysus, you're such a nerd."

"But you love it."

"I love you." He held the back of my head while he leaned in to kiss me. He drew my bottom lip between his teeth, gently tugging and making me moan for more. My hands skimmed under his T-shirt, toying with the line of hair leading under his waistband.

"Do you love me enough to go as Jean in her classic green and yellow bodysuit for my Halloween birthday bash? A guy only turns thirty-two once."

"I'll consider it if you keep kissing me until your parents get home."

My answer came in the form of a smile before I grabbed his waist, flipping us so Dove ended up on his back on the bed. I gave him exactly what he'd asked for, and I vowed to myself that I always would.

EPILOGUE

DUBHLAINN

One Month Later

I T WAS THE MORNING AFTER Mac's birthday, and my fuckin' head felt like it was going to explode. Unlike the holy show of the last time I'd gone to a club with Mac, this time I'd had fun. Too much fun if the knocking in my head was any indication. I'd known in the moment that I was overdoing it—I just hadn't cared. I wore the fuckin' bodysuit, and even padded it and did my makeup. Turning it into a full-drag look gave me never-ending confidence, which contributed in me getting fuckin' mangled. The main cause for my hungover state? Mac. He'd surprised me by wearing some spandex of his own—he went as Cyclops. His muscled body filled the suit out bloody sinfully. I couldn't keep my hands off of him, and since he was the birthday boy, everyone had been buying him—and me by extension —shots.

I don't remember how we got back to our flat. I blacked out way before then and woke up when Mac was stripping me of my suit and completely *un*sexy padding. He hadn't seemed to mind. He took me for a ride then we passed out in a drunken, sweaty heap of limbs and spandex.

A bang followed by cursing in the kitchen had me grinning. I sat up to find painkillers and a glass of water on the nightstand. My grin widened, and I took the tablets before pulling on some pajama pants and one of Mac's zip-up sweaters. It was far too big on me, which made it perfect for the dip in temperature.

The first thing that caught my attention in the kitchen was the absence of music. The second was my fella at the open fridge, slightly bent over in nothing but his kex—looking like the fine thing he was with that gorgeous, round arse on full display. The third thing I noticed was that there was a large blanket draped over the living room furniture—and some of the kitchen chairs were missing.

"What's going on out here?"

Mac spun around, and set the milk on the counter next to two bowls of Froot Loops. "Oh, great—you're awake." He closed the distance between us then gave me a quick peck on the lips while he groped my arse. He pulled back, eyeing his sweater hanging off of me. "I must say, I really do love it when you wear my clothes, although I cranked the heat up, so you might get too hot if you don't get naked."

"I'm sure I'll manage."

He hummed, grinning wolfishly down at me. "You'll come to see things my way soon enough." He kissed the tip of my nose then walked back over to the counter. "To answer your question, I got up early to make breakfast, only to find that I'd forgotten to buy groceries. You made me a list before class yesterday, I know, I know. I'm sorry. I hope Froot Loops are okay for now—we can go out for lunch or supper if you want to."

I swallowed the lump in my throat. "This is perfect." *This is us.* I didn't need anything more than this.

Mac's bright smile made him even more handsome. He poured milk into each of the bowls then handed me one. "How's your head?"

I groaned. "Good call with the painkillers this morning. Thank you."

"I figured. Which is why I built us a cozy blanket fort to block out the light."

"A blanket fort?"

He stared at me blankly then nodded toward the living room. "Do you not build blanket forts in Ireland?"

"I can't speak for the entire country, but no, I never have." I looked at the living room again, and noticed that the coffee table had been pushed aside. It stood to reason that the kitchen chairs and stools must be supporting this blanket fort.

"Good God. Okay, move it along, kiddo. Get in there."

Mac held my bowl for me while I knelt down, lifted one of the edges of the dangling blanket, and crawled under. I was shocked to see he'd set up a dim lantern and padded the floor with the blankets and pillows from my bed. Remembering he was waiting for me, I reached back out and took both bowls, handing one back to him once he was inside sitting next to me.

He took a bite of his cereal, while I was too transfixed by how something so simple could feel so… intimate. "So, what do you think?"

"I think it's great. It feels like we're in our own little private world. I've got everything I need—you even brought the cribbage board and a deck of cards."

He smiled at me again, the corners of his eyes crinkling slightly, and I hoped he'd never stop showing me that smile. "I'm glad you like it."

We finished our breakfast while chatting over our friends' antics last night. Mac had invited Taylor, who also showed up in full drag as Diana Ross. The secret was out to everyone that I was a drag queen, though everyone was nothing but supportive.

"You've got some great friends," I said, settling between Mac's legs. I was turned toward him with my arm around his neck and my legs bent over one of his.

"They're pretty awesome dudes."

"What about Blake?"

"She's an awesome dude too. 'Dude' knows no gender in my vocab," he replied with a smirk.

"Of course you'd say that." A thought suddenly occurred to me. I was sure I already knew the answer, but I still needed to ask him. "Do you usually spend Christmas with your family?"

"Yeah, Christmas is a pretty big holiday for the Buchanan clan. Cousins, aunts, and uncles come out of the woodwork and all that. Why?"

"I was thinking about going home this year. My granny is getting older, and I'd love to see her again. I'd… also like for you to meet her." I held my breath waiting for his reply.

"You want me to come to Ireland with you next month?"

"Aye, I do. I understand if you can't or would rather—"

He literally pinched my lips closed and chuckled. "Don't be silly. I'd love to go with you."

"Really?" I couldn't hide the joyful lilt in my voice, nor did I want to.

"Of course." He said it like it was the most obvious answer. "You're my sexy prince *and* my killer queen; you're everything. I'll gladly go anywhere with you."

I kissed him fiercely, ready to push him down and tear off my clothes—just like the bastard said I would. Damn him.

"Wait," he said seriously. "Does this mean I get to be introduced to a horde of new people as your 'fella'? Because that was pretty awesome last night."

I cringed as memories of me completely langers came flooding back. I'd done just as he'd said, and told anyone who'd listen that Mac was my fella, or sometimes even my handsome fella. My embarrassment melted away when I saw that he was still smiling, not in a teasing way, but completely serious.

"Aye. I'll make sure everyone on the Emerald Isle knows yer mine." I played up my accent for him, knowing it was a guaranteed way to get him going.

Mac flipped me onto my back, attacking me with kisses and caresses. He unzipped my sweater, and flicked his hot tongue over one of my nipples, making me moan in pleasure. As he slowly worked me over, I greedily pawed at him, wanting more. He gave me everything I wanted and more— he always did. Every day with Mac guaranteed laughter and shenanigans, and I couldn't wait to see what tomorrow held for us.

ALSO BY SERENE FRANKLIN

PRINCES

OF

THE

UNIVERSE

Crazy Little Thing Book One

SERENE FRANKLIN

ACKNOWLEDGMENTS

Thanks to all the usual suspects, and Clare. Dove wouldn't have been as Irish without you.

ABOUT THE AUTHOR

Serene Franklin lives in Halifax (Nova Scotia, not California), but has fallen in love with Chicago through research and writing. She has a political science degree, and—more importantly—an adorable and mildly irritating Goldendoodle named Tai.

When not writing, she enjoys reading, cooking spicy food, listening to music, losing at crib, and watching anime. Serene is a proud otaku and collector of anime figures in addition to novels and yaoi manga.

Serene currently writes contemporary MM romance, but has plans to branch out into other subgenres.

Email: sfwrites801@gmail.com

 twitter.com/serenitydarko

 instagram.com/serenity_darko

 bookbub.com/profile/serene-franklin

www.ingramcontent.com/pod-product-compliance
Lightning Source LLC
Chambersburg PA
CBHW032129170626
46808CB00006B/2163